Dear Mystery Reader:

Black Water is the latest in Doug Allyn's excellent series featuring Mitch Mitchell.

If you've read Doug Allyn's previous mysteries, you know *Black Water* will deliver tight plotting and plenty of action. I thought I would draw your attention to the fact that in each of his books, Doug also reflects on some important ideas. It's done ever so skillfully, without didacticism or philosophizing. *Black Water* made me think about how the past influences the present. For many of *Black Water*'s characters, earlier passions are the source for present-day cruelty, rage and crime. In contrast, Mitch's style of facing trouble and loss has produced integrity.

To my mind, this is the best sort of book: a fun read that left me thinking. I hope you enjoy it as much as I did.

Yours in crime,

Dana Edwin Isaacson

Dana Edwin Isaacson
Senior Editor
St. Martin's Dead Letter Paperback Mysteries

ALSO BY DOUG ALLYN

BLACK WATER

DOUG ALLYN

St. Martin's Paperbacks

BLACK WATER

Copyright © 1996 by Doug Allyn.

All rights reserved. No part of this book may be used or reproduced in any manner whatsoever without written permission except in the case of brief quotations embodied in critical articles or reviews. For information address St. Martin's Press, 175 Fifth Avenue, New York, N.Y. 10010.

Library of Congress Catalog Card Number: 95-25854

ISBN: 0-312-96150-2

Printed in the United States of America

St. Martin's Press hardcover edition/April 1996
St. Martin's Paperbacks edition/April 1997

10 9 8 7 6 5 4 3 2 1

A year or so ago, in the early morning hours after an awards banquet, the band was playing its last song to a few clusters of woozy writers while a well-known publisher dozed at his table. Ruth Cavin, my editor and friend, was alone in front of the bandstand, swaying to the beat of the music, her eyes shining.

"Hey," I said, "it's one in the morning. Aren't you just a wee bit bushed?"

"Not at all," she said. "Oh, I know when you look at me, you probably see a little old lady. But I was sixteen once and that girl's still alive and well. In here." She tapped her breast for emphasis.

She was right. When I thought about it, I realized she really is sixteen. Or thereabout.

So, for Ruth, and my wife, Eve, and the other lucky ones who have managed to sneak past the age of consent without surrendering their adolescent hearts . . .

1
THE STRANGER

"UGLY," RED said. "And I mean big-time ugly."

"Could you translate that into English?" I asked. My tone was light, but my heart was sinking. Red was teetering atop a fifteen-foot ladder, carefully examining the roof beams of my lakefront café.

"It looks like dry rot," she said, frowning. "Apparently, the roof's been leaking awhile and the water's been puddling up here on the beams. Grab me an ice pick from behind the bar, please. And toss me up a towel, too. I just washed my hair this morning and the grunge on these beams is older than God."

"Can I let go of the ladder?"

"Hang on a second," Red said. "I want to scramble up here to get a better look anyway."

I held the ladder while Red eased her lanky, muscular frame up onto one of the cross beams that supported the vaulted ceiling. Then I trotted around behind the bar and grabbed an ice pick out of the utensil drawer. The Crow's Nest is an old building, a turn-of-the-century bar/restaurant with a tackle shop attached. I inherited it from my father a year ago. His death caught me by surprise; he was only fifty. But perhaps we're never truly prepared for a death, no matter when. We weren't close, my father and I. At the time of his death in an auto accident, we hadn't spoken in years. I'd always thought we would work out our differences, eventually. I was wrong. We ran out of time.

My father was not a forgiving man, so I was surprised that he left me the Crow's Nest. I was less surprised that his mortgage payments were four months behind. Still, the dining room and the bar have a terrific view of Huron Harbor, and I was ready for a change in my life. And, as a single woman with a young son to support, I've learned to take what comes and make what I can of it.

Red was inching along the cross beam, scowling at the rafter above it where it met the roof and scaring me spitless with every move. She's in her mid-thirties, a handsome, athletic woman, agile as a cougar. She's also my best friend, and it was a very long fall to the hardwood floor. I was so focused on her progress, I nearly skewered my first customer of the day with the ice pick as he stepped through the door.

"Whoa," he said, raising his hands. "I surrender." He was a stranger, a young Latin dude in a dressy leather jacket and fashionably faded jeans. I'm tall for a woman, nearly five nine in my stocking feet. He was six foot plus. I suppose he was also passably attractive, if you're into street-scruffy MTV types.

"Sorry," I said. "We're kind of in the middle of something. I'm afraid the grill isn't open yet."

"Take your time," he said, sauntering to the bar. "I'm in no hurry." He perched on a bar stool and swiveled around to watch.

I climbed back up the ladder and passed Red the ice pick. She made a couple of tentative pokes, then hit a soft spot. The pick disappeared into the wood nearly an inch and a half. "Damn," she said softly. "You might as well take care of our customer, Mitch. If the other beams are as spongy as this one, we're definitely going to need the money."

Up close, the guy at the bar looked better. He was probably in his mid-twenties, with curious brown eyes. His only flaw was a semipermanent pout hiding behind his scruffy goatee.

Ordinarily, I hate tending bar in the mornings. People who

drink before noon are apt to be surly, and since I'm a bit edgy myself early in the morning, it's a bad combination. Red's much better at it, but as an attractive woman who happens to be gay, she's a past master of aggravation management.

Bartending isn't a trade I chose freely. When I took over the Nest, I had visions of spending cheery days in the dive shop renting boats and scuba gear while my son, Corey, played on the beach. It actually worked that way during the summer months. Scuba diving was the trade my father raised me in, so I know the equipment and the jargon. I earned enough in the shop to keep my head above water, so to speak. I also brought in extra cash diving for lost gear on the lake bottom: outboard motors, tackle boxes. And sometimes bodies.

But in the fall, the sunbirds fly south. Diving jobs thin out, but mortgage payments go on forever. My son returned to his private middle school, and I'd been working myself half to death to ease the ache of missing him. I was even desperate enough to tend bar in the mornings.

"What'll you have?" I said, mustering a halfhearted grimace I hoped would pass for a welcome.

"Make it a Wild Turkey, neat."

"A little early, isn't it?" I said it without thinking. I heard a groan from above, but it wasn't the patron saint of bartenders; it was only Red.

The Latin eyed me a moment, and I braced myself for a blast of static, but he just shrugged. "Yes, ma'am, I guess it is. Do me a Coke instead. Do you know a guy named Owen McClain?"

"I know who he is," I said, parking a Coke in front of him.

"In a little town like this, I expect everybody knows everybody, right?"

"More or less," I said.

He waited a beat. "So? What can you tell me about him?"

"Not very much. In small towns, folks tend to look out for one another. I know who Owen is; I even know some of his friends. I don't know you."

"Calderon," he said. "Jimmy Calderon. You?"

"Michelle Mitchell," I said. "People call me Mitch."

"Okay, Mitch, I'm not a friend of Mr. McClain's exactly. More like a . . . distant relative. Why don't you tell me what you know about him? And here's a little something for your trouble." He laid a five on the bar.

I was wearing my morning work grubbies, jeans and a Michigan State sweatshirt. Maybe I looked like somebody with a five-dollar price tag. I dug in my pocket, found a quarter, and dropped it on his five. "There's a pay phone by the door," I said. "If Owen's in the book, I'm sure he'll be glad to hear from a . . . relative." Again I waited for some guff. But he just smiled, picked up the quarter, then slid off his bar stool and strolled to the phone. He left the five on the bar.

"Thunder Bay Drive?" he said, scanning the book. "Where's that?"

"A mile or so down the lakeshore," I said. "But I imagine he'll be at the plant. McClain Industrial Fuels."

"Yeah? He own the place, does he?"

"I really couldn't say," I said.

"Right." He nodded. "Small towns. Thanks, Mitch, you've been a big help. Maybe after I get settled in we can go out some time. Have dinner, a few laughs. I'll give you a jingle." And he sauntered out, cocky as a goose the day after Christmas.

I walked to the end of the bar and watched him get into a tan Ford Escort with airport-rental plates. Odd. He didn't strike me as the tourist type. He gunned the Escort out of the lot like a teenybopper showing off for his buddies. I thought about giving Owen McClain a call, but what would I say? Somebody asked about you? The guy seemed harmless, and frankly, I had troubles of my own.

"Can you drag the ladder over here, please?" Red called from the far end of the room.

"Finished already?" I said, sliding the ladder beneath the beam Red was perched on.

"*Finished* may be the right word," Red said grimly. "I'm no expert, Mitch, but it looks like a leaky roof's the least of your

4

problems. At least half of the rafter beams have dry rot."

"Can they be repaired?"

"I doubt it," she said, stepping carefully from the cross beam to the ladder. "Maybe a few can be salvaged, but most of them will have to be replaced. I know more about boats than buildings, Mitch, but if the Nest was a ship, we'd be lowering the lifeboats."

"What lifeboats?" I asked.

2
HARD CASH

I KNEW I'd have to grovel; to fall on my bended knees and plead for a loan with some nasty little twerp with dandruff and a green eyeshade. I was wrong. The loan officer at the Huron Harbor branch of Michigan National Bank was blond, thirtyish, plump, and, by my best guesstimate, roughly seven months pregnant. I didn't find her condition much comfort. I tried to recall what my own moods had been like when I was seven months along with Corey. The only things that bubbled to mind were impatience and a major-league case of the surlies.

Her clothes were encouraging, though. We were nearly a match. She was wearing a gray-green tweed skirt, a ruffled peasant blouse, plastic pearls. I'd chosen a Donna Karan navy skirt, white blouse, pumps and purse to match. No jewelry. My no-nonsense businesswoman's disguise.

"Hi," she said, offering her hand, "I'm Ellen Maybry, Miss Mitchell. My husband and I met for lunch several times on the new deck you added to the Nest this summer. It was a wonderful idea."

"Glad you enjoyed it," I said, feeling a trace more comfortable, though still a little exposed. Her office faced the lobby of the bank and the door was open.

"We did. Very much." She nodded, flipping through the pages of the paperwork I'd completed two days earlier. "As to your application, the figures you show here are encouraging. I see business slowed a bit in September, but that's normal for northern Michigan. It looks like you've got a good shot at turning the Crow's Nest into a going concern. But . . . there are also a few problems."

"That's why I'm here," I said, keeping my tone neutral.

"Right," she said, nodding. "And solving problems is our business, in a manner of speaking. Would you mind closing the office door?"

"That bad, huh?" I said, swinging the door shut behind me.

"I hope not, but privacy in a small town's hard to come by. For openers, let me say that while my first loyalty is obviously to the bank, I'm not your adversary here. I'd like to see more women in business do well. That said, let's get right to what I see as the difficulties. Do you mind if I speak frankly?"

"Please do," I said.

"The final decision on any loan rests with the board, of course, but I can tell you that, as it stands, your application's unlikely to be approved at this time. One problem is the period of ownership. You've owned the business only a little over a year, and it's hard to gauge your long-term prospects on that basis."

"I've been making a profit almost from the beginning," I countered.

"Granted, and that's definitely in your favor. It looks like you can manage the payments all right, but that's not the central difficulty. The problem is the type of loan you need. The Crow's Nest is an older building. The dry rot you mentioned may be limited to the area you plan to replace, but we really can't be sure how extensive either the rot or the repairs will be until the project is actually under way. If you have to replace the roof and the support beams, you could be looking at thirty to forty thousand, minimum, and frankly, your collateral can't carry that. Do you have any assets you haven't listed?"

"No," I said. "My financial life's story is right in front of you."

7

"I see. Well, then the obvious alternative would be to find someone who'd be willing to cosign your note—a relative, or perhaps a friend, with assets that would cover the loan."

"A sugar daddy?" I said.

"I beg your pardon?"

"Thanks for your time," I said, rising abruptly. "I guess I'll have to find some other way."

"Miss Mitchell, please wait. I didn't mean to offend you."

"No? If you read my application, you know that I've been supporting myself and my son on my own for the past ten years by working as a maintenance diver on oil platforms in the Texas Gulf. My job paid well, but as a single woman, I still had a tough time getting credit, so I've always been careful with it. I make payments on time; I've never bounced a check or even maxed out a charge card. But now that I need a business loan, I suddenly need someone else to sign on the dotted line for me?"

"It's not that, believe me. I know how hard it is for a woman alone—I've been there myself. I give you my word this is no reflection on you personally. Your credit rating is excellent. The only problem here is the shortage of collateral for what could turn out to be a fairly large loan. I simply suggested a cosigner as one option."

"Sorry," I said, easing back into the chair. "Maybe I'm a little touchy on the subject. If I overreacted, I apologize, but I'm not sure it matters. Offhand, I can't think of a soul I can hit on for a spare forty grand, so where does this leave me?"

"In kind of a tough spot, I'm afraid," she said. "To get the kind of financing you need, you'll either have to come up with substantially more collateral or a cosigner with assets enough to cover the debt. And with the kind of roof damage you've described, it's even possible the building could flunk its next safety inspection. When were you inspected last?"

"A little while after I took over the Nest, a year or so ago. The guy didn't check the roof, though; he basically just strolled through the place and okayed it."

"A typical north-country inspection," she said wryly. "Once

8

around lightly and a beer to cut the dust. Technically, they're supposed to inspect businesses open to the public on a yearly basis, but the county only has a couple of inspectors and they're usually six to eight months behind. According to the building codes, the kind of structural problems you mentioned could get you closed down, but the Nest has been open for a hundred years or so. It should hold together long enough for you to work this out."

"I hope so." I sighed, rising to leave. "To be honest, I'm not sure I came to the right place for help."

"How do you mean?"

"I passed at least two churches on the way here," I said. "Maybe I should have stopped in and lit a candle or something. Because if I need to find collateral for forty grand, I don't need a bank. I need a miracle."

3
HOOKED

"WHAT DO you mean he walked on water?" I asked.

"Exactly that," Sheriff Bauer said blandly, leaning on the bar. "Huey LeBlanc was fishing below the Narrows Dam. A flat-lander from Toledo asked him where the bass were bitin', so Huey tells him to wade out in the channel till he feels the footing slope away, then drop his hook. Only the guy just kept walking, six, seven feet out. The water was barely over his ankles and the channel's at least ten foot deep there. Huey swears he thought it was the Second Coming. The guy was honest-to-God walking on water."

"What's the joke, Charlie?" I said. "You'd need stilts to walk more than a foot out from that bank."

"Unfortunately, it's no joke, Mitch. There's a car in the river. It's apparently jammed crossways in the channel. The guy from Toledo walked up the trunk and onto the roof, then just stood there. And old Huey almost had a heart attack."

"If the car's so near the surface, why didn't Huey spot it?"

"It's black water there. River silt's all roiled up from the dam spillways upstream. I couldn't see the car even after Huey showed me exactly where it was. Had to poke around with a fishing rod to be sure he wasn't pulling my leg. I need a diver to

10

check out the vehicle and hook up a towline to it, Mitch, some-body who can work blind," Charlie said carefully, avoiding my eyes. "Know anybody who can use a quick seventy-five bucks?"

I glanced around the Nest. There were a few scuba divers in the club—we do a good lakefront trade. But there was no one I'd want to send into black water. It's an ugly, dangerous job, definitely not for amateurs. And Charlie knew it, too. Which is why he didn't ask me to do it directly. Not because I'm a woman; Charlie and I have worked together before and he knows I'm good at my trade. But we're also friends, and he wouldn't want me to take on a risky job out of friendship. Charlie's a genuine old-fashioned gentleman. He's big-boned, freckled, and likable, and a dozen years older than I am. Sometimes I wish he was my type. Whatever that is. Life's never that simple.

"I know one heckuva diver who might be interested if the county would up the price to a hundred," I said.

"Then let's make it an even hundred and twenty," Charlie said. "Need any help with your gear?"

4

NIGHT AND THE RIVER

THE SUN was setting as Charlie Bauer cautiously guided his blue sheriff's department Blazer down the embankment to the narrow shelf of the Odawa River's floodplain. The wrecker was already there, backed up to the river's edge. Biff Kowalski was stalking around his huge blue GMC 7500, stomping his greasy engineer's boots into the soft clay of the bank. Biff's as solidly built as his tow truck and weighs nearly as much. He's usually a mild-tempered sort, placid as a side of beef and only slightly brighter. But he definitely knows his business: trucks and tow bars and winches, and in this case, rivers. He looked worried. And anything that worried Biff definitely worried me.

"I don't like this one damn bit, Charlie," Biff said, chewing a corner of his lip. "Current's awful fast here. When the car comes outta the muck, it's gonna have one helluva lot of water leanin' on it. If the car's big enough, it could maybe burn out my bull winch or even drag my wrecker in after it. I've seen it happen."

"Mitch'll find out what kind of car we're dealing with while she's down there," Charlie said. "If you think it's too heavy for your rig, we'll call out another wrecker to back you up, okay? Now stand next to me, give a lady some privacy."

12

Charlie and Biff stood together with their backs to the Blazer to shield me from the gawkers along the road as I slid out of my jeans and got ready for the river. Charlie's courtesy wasn't really necessary. I was wearing a swimsuit, but the people up on the shoulder wouldn't know that, and as I said, Charlie Bauer is a very old-fashioned guy.

I put on a "woolly bear" suit of long underwear first, then climbed into a Farmer John–style foam-neoprene wet suit topped by a hooded vest. The kibitzers up by the road were probably making wisecracks about women overdressing, but working in river current is like standing in front of an air conditioner going full blast. The constant flow of the water can bring on hypothermia in a matter of minutes. The worst of it is, if you're busy, you don't realize what's happening. The gradual chill makes you stupid and clumsy before you know it, and in black water, stupid and clumsy will kill you quicker than Bonnie and Clyde.

When I stepped out of the vehicle, I got a smattering of applause from the peanut gallery along the road, and I gave 'em a quick bow. I popped open the Blazer's tailgate, then hesitated.

Something was odd. I glanced back up at the motley line of spectators, and spotted the young Latin I'd met in the Nest the week before. What was his name? Calderon? He'd cleaned himself up. He was wearing a dark blazer and tie and he'd shaved off the ratty goatee. Maybe he really was a relative and the Mc-Clains had taken him in. Surprise, surprise.

Back to business. I strapped on a lightweight backpack with a single thirty-minute air tank, opting for maneuverability over dive time. My gear belt held a lifeline on a reel, two flashlights, and I had a helmet light as well, powered by a belt-mounted battery pack. I didn't bother with flippers; I just slipped on a pair of canvas deck shoes. I'd be wading down there, not swimming. I double-checked my regulator, then joined Charlie at the river's edge and handed him the end of my lifeline.

"Three hard tugs if I've got trouble. Five if I want you to haul me out. How do you want to work this?"

13

"You know the drill. Check for a body first. If you find one, come on out and we'll see about getting the spillways closed to get a better look at the scene. If the car's empty, find out what you can about it, make, model, whatever. Then come up for the cable and we'll haul it out of there. And Mitch, be careful, okay? Biff's right—last week's rain has the river up and the current's nasty here."

"Right." I waded a few steps downstream, then stepped away from the bank. Even with the water only waist-deep, the pressure from the river was a living thing, tugging at my legs, trying to pull me out into the main thrust of the current. I felt a roller-coaster rush of adrenaline—excitement, tempered by fear. This one would be interesting.

I moved cautiously upstream, groping blindly in the murk ahead until I touched metal. I ran my hands quickly over it, tracing its contours. It was the rounded edge of the trunk. The car was nose-down in the riverbed and I was on the driver's side. I braced myself, leaned against the car, then pushed as hard as I could on the rear fender. It didn't even quiver. I couldn't budge it. It was bedded firmly in the muck. Good. The greatest danger in a dive like this is having the vehicle shift at a bad time and getting pinned under it. This one was solid as a stone elephant.

Using the car's body to shield myself from the current, I slipped under the surface. Absolute blackness. Not a hint of light. I switched on my helmet lamp, but it only haloed off the turbid silt. Whiteout instead of blackout. No help at all. I switched it off and worked blind, feeling my way along the side of the car.

Roofline, rear window . . . and then a gap. The driver's door was open. Damn. This would make it trickier. If the car had been closed up, the silt would have settled out of the water inside and I could have scanned the interior with a light. As it was, the only way to locate a body in there was by touch. I felt an icy chill that had nothing to do with the river current.

If you have to kiss a frog, don't look at it too long. Grasping the steering wheel with my left hand, I quickly ran my right hand over the front seat, the ceiling, the dashboard, the floor. Nothing. I inched farther inside, reached around the front seat, and groped blindly in the back. I began on the ceiling, slid my hand across until I felt the backseat, then down. . . . Something spongy moved beneath my hand!

I recoiled, banging the back of my head against the front door frame. Damn! My eyes felt as if they were pressed against the Lexan lens of my face mask. But there was nothing to see. Black water. I tried to remember what . . . whatever I'd touched felt like. Cloth. A sleeve perhaps? With an arm in it? I wasn't sure.

Damn it, damn it, damn it. In this murk, I couldn't even check my watch to see how long I'd been down here. Not long enough. Nowhere near thirty minutes. I had no excuse to surface. Pity. I had a memory flash of a comedian . . . George Carlin? Talking about being on an airplane and seeing flames coming out of an engine. But he couldn't bring himself to ask the stewardess about it. Because he'd rather die than look like a schmuck.

It was funny because it was true. And the truth was, frightened or not, I wasn't about to surface and tell Sheriff Bauer or Biff that there *might* be a body in this godforsaken car. Neither one would say anything. But they'd think it. Next time, better get a man for the job.

I swallowed hard and reached into the rear passenger area. And brushed against the cloth. And felt it give. It was too late to back off now. I squeezed, gently at first, then harder. The fabric pinched together. Not a sleeve, or a coat . . . the material was too coarse. More like . . . Hell, it was carpeting. The carpet from the rear floor had bubbled up and I was holding a piece of it.

I ran my hand quickly over it, far enough to know there were no more surprises. And then I backed out and surfaced, letting Charlie pull me close enough to the bank to stand.

I spat out my mouthpiece. "Nobody home. I can't tell what kind of a car it is—can't see an inch down there. I could reach clear across to the far door, though, so it must be a compact. Should I hook it up?"

"You want to take a break first?" Charlie said, concerned. "You sound a little shaky."

"It's cold as a witch's kiss down there, that's all," I said curtly. "I'm okay."

"You're the boss," Charlie said, mildly exasperated. Biff grinned and handed me the hook on the end of the cable and reeled a few feet off the winch. I replaced my mouthpiece, stepped off the bank, and slid back down into the blackness. I felt along the car till I found the rear wheel, then beyond it to the frame. I looped the line around a solid crossmember, hooked up, then backed out and surfaced again. Charlie gave me a hand up.

"Everything set?"

I nodded, not trusting my voice yet. Biff pulled down the power arm on his winch and began reeling in the cable. The big drum seemed to hesitate a moment when the cable hit dead level, and the wrecker shuddered, rocking on its tandem wheels. Then with a deep, liquid gurgle, the river muck released its hold and the car began inching slowly out of the black water and up the bank.

When the rear wheels crawled clear of the river and I was sure I wouldn't have to go back down, I trudged over to Charlie's Blazer and shed my air-tank backpack and tool belt. And I took a moment to think about how ugly it had been to feel that damned piece of carpet. And how good it felt not to quit. A little private "attagirl." The best kind.

When I turned back, the car was already two-thirds clear of the river. Coffee-colored water gushed out of the open door and river silt slid down the roof and the sides.

The steel cable had crushed part of the bumper assembly, popping the trunk, but the car was easily recognizable. And it looked familiar. It was an airport-rental Ford Escort—tan.

Charlie was checking the license plate against his clipboard. "Gotcha," he said.

"Were you looking for this one?" I asked.

"It was on the hot sheet," he nodded. "Guy took it on a three-day rental at the airport a week or so ago and didn't return it."

"A young guy? Latin?" I asked.

He glanced at the sheet, then at me. "Yeah. Name was Calderon. What are you, a witch?"

"Absolutely," I said. "But not this time. I met him last week at the Nest. In fact, if you'd like to talk to him, I spotted him earlier standing with the rubberneckers up on—there. See the tall guy on the end, the one in the blue sport coat? He's your man."

5
CALDERON REDUX

"Yo!" CHARLIE shouted. "Hey, you! The guy on the end? Could you come down here a minute, please?"

Calderon hesitated, then stepped over the railing and clambered down the bank. He was carrying a flight bag, and as he entered the ring of light from the wrecker's halogen roof rack, I realized I'd made a mistake. There was a strong resemblance all right, but it wasn't the same man. This one was older, a little more solidly built. And better-looking.

"My diver here thinks there's a chance you might be able to tell us something about this car," Charlie said.

"I'm afraid I don't understand," Calderon said.

"I'm sorry," I put in. "It was my mistake. From a distance, you looked a lot like the guy who rented this car."

"You mean Jimmy Calderon? You're saying this is his car?"

Charlie nodded. "A James Calderon rented it. You know him?"

"I'm Ray Calderon. Jimmy's my younger brother," he said, stalking grimly over to the dripping car. "How did it get in the river?"

"I was hoping you could tell us," Charlie said.

"No, I don't know anything about this. I just flew in. I told the airport cabbie to take me to your office, but as we drove past, he said it looked like the whole department was down here, so we stopped."

"Why were you looking for me?" Charlie asked.

"My brother came here on . . . business, last week. He was supposed to stay in touch. When he didn't, I got worried."

"Where are you from, Mr. Calderon?" Charlie asked.

"Virginia. Norfolk. I got out of the navy a few months ago."

"A long way to come," Charlie said. "Why didn't you just telephone?"

Calderon hesitated a moment, then shrugged. "Because if Jimmy was all right, I didn't want to cause any fuss."

"You mean because your brother's on parole," Charlie said. "I ran a check on him when his car went overdue. Armed robbery, wasn't it?"

"It sounds worse than it was," Calderon said evenly. "He's young; he made some mistakes. He's paid for them."

"Not entirely, or he wouldn't still be on parole. Let me ask you a question, Mr. Calderon, straight up. What are the chances your brother ditched this car in the river and skipped?"

"No way," Calderon said positively. "He only had six months of parole left and he had a good job. He had no reason to run."

"He didn't have permission to leave Virginia, either, but he did."

"Charlie?" Biff interrupted. "I'm hooked up and ready to haul 'er to the yard. You want the stuff in the trunk?"

"What stuff?"

"Luggage," Biff said. "A couple of suitcases."

"Suitcases?" Charlie said. We followed him over to the car. The front end was a foot off the ground, but the trunk was still open. Calderon pulled one of the muddy suitcases out, laid it on the ground, and popped the catches, opening it.

"These are Jimmy's all right," he said grimly, sorting quickly through the sodden clothing. "This is a picture of my . . . our mother," he said, handing a photograph in a K Mart frame to Charlie. "You still think he dumped the car and took off, Sheriff? Without his clothes?"

"Probably not," Charlie conceded. "On the other hand, I can't say I like the alternative any better."

"What do you mean?"

"We had a hard rain most of last week, Mr. Calderon, and the riverbank's so muddied up, we can't be sure exactly where the car went in. See that area up there, just before the bridge? It's a blind curve, a nasty one. People miss it sometimes, mostly out-of-towners who don't know the road. It's especially difficult to see in the rain. And with the bank as muddy as it is, a car'd skid down it like a toboggan and into the river. Then the current would probably carry it to roughly the point where we hauled it out."

"And you think my brother missed a curve in the dark and wound up in the river?"

"It kinda looks like it. Let's say it happened that way. If he got out all right, he'd probably only have the clothes he was wearing and whatever money he had on him. Assuming he didn't report the accident because he didn't want to risk being picked up for violating his parole, what do you think he'd do?"

"He'd call me," Ray said slowly. "He'd have to. But he didn't. You think he's still in the river, don't you?"

"No, sir, I'm not saying that. We don't know what occurred yet. I just want you to be aware of the possibility."

"I see." Calderon nodded. He walked away from us to the water's edge, staring out into the dark, his hands thrust deep in his pockets, his shoulders hunched against the pain.

"But if um . . . if that's what happened, where's the body?"

"The driver's door was open," I said reluctantly.

"But damn it, Jimmy's a strong swimmer, and that car was only a few feet from the bank."

"That's where it came to rest," Charlie said. "More than likely went in about fifty yards upstream. He could have been injured

20

in the crash, or maybe he simply couldn't find the bank in the rain."

"I . . . suppose that's possible," Calderon said, nodding. "All right, where would a body end up if it went into the water here?"

"The river empties into Lake Huron about four hundred yards downstream," I said. "The thrust of the current continues quite a distance offshore. With the water this high, it might be active a mile and a half out, maybe even two miles."

"Bodies surface after a day or so," Calderon said, his voice barely audible. "Wouldn't someone have found it by now?"

"In the summer, maybe," Charlie said, "when we have a lot of boaters. But this time of year, especially with all the rain this past week, it's quite possible it wouldn't be seen. We can start an air search tomorrow, but it's a big lake out there, Mr. Calderon, a hundred and fifty miles to the Canadian shore. And it's been a week. He might not be on the surface anymore. But maybe we're being too hasty here. Why don't we consider some other possibilities."

"Like what?"

"I don't know, but maybe you do. Why did your brother come up to Huron Harbor?"

"It was . . . personal. He was . . . um, he was trying to locate his father."

"His father?" I said, surprised.

"That's right," Calderon said, looking at me for the first time. "We're only half brothers, Jimmy and I—same mother, different fathers. Our mother never married Jimmy's father and Jimmy never had any contact with him. He came up here to find him."

"Who's his father?" Charlie asked.

"A man named Owen McClain."

"Then he made a trip for nothing," Charlie said. "The only Owen McClain I know's in his early thirties."

"He did ask about Owen," I put in.

"You talked to my brother?" Calderon asked, surprised. "When?"

21

"Last . . . Wednesday, I think," I said, glancing at Charlie for an okay. "I own a little bar and restaurant and he stopped in for . . . information, mostly. I told him he'd probably find Owen at the fuels plant. And he drove off in that direction when he left."

"Well, we can't do any more here tonight," Charlie said. "Maybe we can get a line on his movements. The McClain place is on the way back to the station anyway. Where can I contact you, Mr. Calderon?"

"No place—I mean, I'm not staying anywhere yet. The cabbie dropped me here. Can I catch a ride into town with you?"

"No problem," Charlie said. "Climb aboard. Passenger side, please. Mitch needs the backseat to change."

6
THE MCCLAINS

"THAT WAS a nice bit of diving you did back there," Calderon said over his shoulder without turning his head. He was riding shotgun in Charlie Bauer's county Blazer. I was in the backseat. I'd shucked my diving gear and climbed back into faded jeans, a sweatshirt, and running shoes.

"Just another day at the office," I said.

"Did you learn in the military?"

"No, I grew up underwater. My dad owned the Crow's Nest and rented boats and diving gear. He taught me. After high school, I got a job with Exxon out on the Texas Gulf for a while, doing underwater maintenance off the oil platforms."

"I didn't know they hired women for that kind of work."

"They don't hire women," I said evenly. "They hire divers who can do the job. The money was good, but the platforms aren't much of a life. My son was in boarding school and I could only see him on weekends. So we moved back up here."

"I can see why," Calderon said absently. "It's beautiful country, what I've seen of it."

"What did you do in the navy, Mr. Calderon?" Charlie asked.

"Flight crew. The last few years, I worked in an air/sea rescue squadron out of Norfolk. Which means I'm aware of the odds against recovering my brother's . . . body. *If* he went into that river."

That thought chilled the coversation until we pulled into the long circular drive of the McClain estate. It's a Tudor-style manor, three stories, probably a dozen rooms or so, overlooking the north shore of Thunder Bay. In Detroit or Grosse Pointe, it would have been surrounded by spear-tipped steel fences, but up here, a low hedge and neighbors are all you need.

I expected Charlie to tell us to wait in the car, but he didn't. Calderon and I flanked him while he rang the buzzer. Chimes tinkled like Waterford crystal somewhere within.

The door was opened by an over-the-hill surfer, or at least that was my first impression. He was tall and tan, a bodybuilder type, mid-forties, with a shoulder-length mane of tousled dark hair. He was wearing a white cable-knit sweater, white slacks, and deck shoes, no socks. No underwear, either, unless I was greatly mistaken. His sleepy gray eyes blinked to instant alert at the sight of Charlie's uniform.

"Yes?"

"I'm Sheriff Bauer. Is Mr. McClain in?"

"Um, of course. This way, please."

We trailed the surfer down a tiled entry hall into a modest-sized living room, comfortably furnished with wine-toned leather sofas and a half dozen chairs. The McClain family was all there, what there is of it. Owen, a pudgy jock gone to seed, had thinning sandy hair and was wearing the vest and dress pants of a business suit; a *Wall Street Journal* rested on his lap. He seemed a solid, stolid citizen. But I noticed his fingertips were raw, nails chewed to the quick, and his skin had a pasty, unhealthy pallor.

His wife, Hannah, stood behind his chair, wary as a doe in a rainstorm. She was a rangy blond stunner, half a head taller than Owen, a local girl, née Luebner. She came from a clan of woodcutters—"cedar savages" in northern Michigan argot—a ragtag army of kids and hounds, pickup trucks and chain saws. I had vague memories of her from high school: a quiet girl with

24

natural good looks, but a little self-conscious about her diction, I thought. She got adequate grades and made the state finals as a distance runner. When she married Owen, the local gentry clucked that he'd married beneath himself. Personally, I thought he'd scored a terrific catch. I wasn't so sure she had.

She was dressed casually in a teal designer sweater, slacks, and pumps, yet she seemed uncomfortable, as if she feared Charlie'd come to haul her back to Shacktown. Heck, maybe she was hoping he would.

Owen's mother, Audrey McClain, was in her wheelchair near the fire. She was tiny, as frail as smoke, probably mid-fifties, but her debility made her seem older. Her pixie-cut platinum hair contrasted with a simple blouse of raw silk, black, with matching skirt, a string of pearls at her throat.

With her finely sculpted face, she must have been strikingly lovely once. To me, she still was. Her shoulders were humped from an injury that forced her to cock her head when she looked at you, like a kitten, listening. Her eyes were catlike too, bright and curious and alert. Her body was bent, but her spirit was unbroken. Rumor said she had a tongue like a horse whip when crossed. I didn't doubt it.

"So, Charlie," she said. "Come to write me up for my various sins, have you?"

"No, ma'am, there's been an accident. A young fella's come up missing. I'm trying to trace his movements, hoping to get a line on him."

"Who's missing?" Owen frowned. "And why come here?"

"His name's James Calderon. He's this gentleman's brother," Charlie added, nodding at Ray. "Thing is, he apparently came to town looking for you, Owen. He may have gone out to the plant. Did you talk to him? Would have been last Wednesday, most likely."

"Wednesday?" Owen blinked uneasily, glancing at his mother. "Yes, I did talk to him for a few minutes. He wasn't making much sense, though. He was babbling something about being my brother, but one of the chippers was down on the shop

25

floor and I was busy as hell. I told him to take a walk, that I didn't have time for games. He got a little pushy, so my uncle Gordon showed him the door. That was about it."

"He said he was your brother and you didn't take time to talk to him?" Charlie said, his tone neutral.

"What was I supposed to do? I'd never seen the guy before in my life, and I couldn't very well let fifty guys stand around at ten bucks an hour while I bat the breeze with some con artist I never heard of. It was all a crock anyway. He was just looking for a handout."

"Actually, he wasn't," Audrey said, cocking her head to gauge Charlie's reaction. "At least he didn't ask me for anything when I talked to him. He just wanted to meet his father."

"He came here to the house?" Charlie asked. "When was that, Mrs. McClain?"

"Late Wednesday afternoon, around four, I think. He apparently got our address out of the phone book."

"Mother," Owen began, but she cut him off with a wave.

"Don't lecture me, Owney. I know I shouldn't have let him in, but it was Ross's day off and I was bored. And he seemed harmless enough."

"What happened?" Charlie prompted.

"At first he said he was a friend of Owney's from out of town, which I knew wasn't true. He was far too interesting to be one of Owney's friends. He asked a few questions about the family, to confirm things in his own mind, I suppose, and then he told me straight out that he was Owney's half brother, that my late husband had an affair with his mother, and that . . . he was the result. He even had pictures to prove it."

"What kind of pictures?" Charlie asked.

"Nothing pornographic, I'm afraid," Audrey said dryly. "Just snapshots of Owen Senior and . . . a very pretty young woman with dark eyes and dark hair. Owen always had excellent taste. One picture was a group shot with a young boy, this gentleman here, unless I'm greatly mistaken."

Calderon nodded but said nothing.

"When I explained that Owen senior died in Vietnam, he . . . well, he was very disappointed, naturally. We chatted awhile, had a drink or two to toast our mutual misfortunes, and then Megan Lundy stopped by to talk about the Arts Council scholarships. And so I . . . gave Mr. Calderon some money, and he left."

"You gave him money?" Owen echoed.

"Not a lot of money, dear, a few hundred. His airfare, more or less. He'd come such a long way for nothing. I felt it was the least I could do. We can afford it. Or rather, *I* can," she added pointedly.

"That's not true," Ray Calderon said slowly.

"Mr. Calderon," Charlie began, "I know this isn't easy for you, but—"

"Easy's got nothing to do with it," Calderon said coolly. "I don't know how much of what this nice lady just told us is true, but I know part of it isn't. Jimmy's father didn't die in Vietnam. He was never there, and Jimmy knew it. So what kind of a game are you running, lady? What the hell's going on here?"

"I've heard enough of this," Owen said, rising, his face flushing. "Charlie, you're out of line bringing this . . . gentleman into my home. I want him gone, now. If you've got any more questions, call my office during business hours. Or talk to my attorney. Ross, show these *people* out, please."

"There's no need to be unpleasant, Owen," Audrey McClain said sharply. "And since I'm the only one who can actually help here, why don't you and Hannah go on to your chamber of commerce meeting? I'll be fine," she said, waving off his objections. "If Charlie hauls out a rubber hose, I'll have Ross throw him out. Or try to. It might be fun to watch. You go on. I'll talk to you later."

"Your mom's right, Owney," Hannah McClain said suddenly, the first time she'd spoken. "We're already running late, and you're supposed to talk about the plant expansion. We'd better go."

Owen hesitated, whipsawed between the two women in his

27

life. "All right," he said reluctantly. "But damn it, Charlie, you keep this short, understand? Mom's been known to overestimate her stamina." He turned and stalked out without another word. Hannah and Audrey exchanged a wry glance of shared amusement and irritation. Then Hannah followed her husband out.

"Well," Audrey said, taking a deep breath, "Ross, I think I'd like a whiskey sour. Anyone else? Miss Mitchell? Coffee? Tea? Something to eat, perhaps?" No one spoke. "Then just get mine, please, Ross. And Ross? Take your time. And knock before you enter, dear." The bodybuilder nodded mutely and trudged off. He left the door ajar. Charlie closed it.

"Please sit down, all of you," Audrey said. "Looking up at you is giving me a stiff neck."

"Mrs. McClain, it's getting late; perhaps tomorrow would be better," Charlie said.

"No, I'd rather get this over and done with now," Audrey said. "I'd like to help this young man if I can. None of this is his fault, after all. But I'm afraid we're into a . . . touchy situation here. He's quite right, actually—my husband, Owen, didn't die in Vietnam. He deserted to avoid serving there, which is why Owney's a bit sensitive on the subject of his father, as you may have gathered. It was a relatively minor scandal at the time; a lot of young men . . . did what they had to in order to avoid the war. Still, my father-in-law was an old-fashioned type, and when he told people that Owen had died in Vietnam, no one bothered to contradict him. Or dared to. Old Harry was a formidable man. By now, I imagine most people believe it actually happened. Owney may half-believe it himself. But . . . you're right, Mr. Calderon," she said, swiveling her chair to face him. "Your brother didn't accept the family cover story. He even showed me a photostat of an army arrest warrant. Which surprised me. I thought President Carter's amnesty took care of all that."

"The amnesty was for draft resisters," Calderon said, "not deserters. Or thieves."

"Thieves?" Charlie echoed.

"There was a . . . misunderstanding about some money

28

Owen took from his unit when he left," Audrey said. "Not much, a few thousand. And I believe a man was injured in the incident. My father-in-law offered to repay every cent of the money when the military police came here making inquiries. I was quite ill at the time. I don't know if he actually did so."

"It wouldn't have mattered, ma'am," Calderon said grimly. "It wasn't just the money. When Captain McClain got orders for Vietnam, he skipped out with his outfit's payroll. A sergeant tried to stop him and your husband shot him for his trouble. The man's still crippled and the charges against your husband are attempted murder, as well as desertion. There's no statute of limitations on charges like those. The army would still like to talk to your husband about it."

"Then they'll need a . . . channeler? Is that the word?" Audrey said. "Owen may not have died in Vietnam, but he is dead. My late father-in-law tried very hard to locate him after the amnesty—police, detectives, attorneys, the works. They found exactly nothing. Not a trace. In the end, we took legal action to have Owen declared dead so Owney could inherit his share of the business. It was not a step we took lightly."

"Having him declared dead may have simplified your personal situation," Calderon said. "It doesn't make any difference to the military. It's still an open case as far as they're concerned."

"Your brother said something along those lines," Audrey said, craning her neck to see him better. "He thought Owen came back here all those years ago. Is that what your mother told him?"

"That's right."

"Well, perhaps she thought so, but it simply wasn't true. Wherever he ran to, it wasn't here. He went off to the army and never came home. Like so many others in those days."

"There's big difference between those others and your husband, Mrs. McClain," Calderon said. "He was never in combat. What makes you so certain he's dead?"

"For one thing, a small army of detectives found no trace of him. But mostly because of the money," she said. "Owen was

29

never good with money. He never had to be. I wasn't surprised when the investigators told me he took some. I'm sure he meant to pay it back. The family could afford it. The point is, the few thousand he took wouldn't have lasted him for very long. He used to spend more than that at his tailor's at a single fitting. But he never contacted us to ask for more. We've never heard from him again. Ever."

"Or so you say, ma'am. No offense, but he *was* your husband, after all."

"You seem like an astute young man," Audrey said, her voice chilling a bit. "Your brother showed me a picture of your mother. She was lovely. If you were Owen, would you have chosen to run off with her? Or come home to . . . this?" She indicated herself and the chair with a flutter of her hand.

"But he didn't run off with my mother. He abandoned her."

"Well, perhaps we made the same mistake, she and I. Apparently, we were both pregnant at the time, and I can tell you from my first experience that Owen, like most men, had no patience with pregnancy. No offense, but perhaps he replaced your mother, as she replaced me. Who can say? But I'm afraid that's really all I can tell you, Mr. Calderon. Your brother left here late in the afternoon. It was raining hard, he was upset, and we'd . . . um, we'd had several brandies together, drowning our sorrows. Perhaps I shouldn't have let him go. But I was more than a little upset myself. I'm sorry."

"I'm sorry, too, ma'am," Calderon said. "For all of it. Thanks for . . . well, for telling me."

"That's quite all right," Mrs. McClain said, "but if you don't mind, I'm a bit tired now."

"Of course," Charlie said, rising. "We'll see ourselves out." He strode quickly to her chair, bent down, and gave her a peck on the forehead. "If you think of anything else that might help, anything at all, please give me a call."

"I will, dear." She nodded. "You take care. Miss?" she said, suddenly turning to me. "You're Shannon Mitchell's daughter, aren't you?"

"Yes," I said, surprised that she knew.

"I wonder, could you stay a minute? I'd like to talk to you. Please."

"I don't know," I said, glancing at Charlie for advice, but his square, freckled face was professionally neutral, unreadable—as usual.

"I'll see that she gets home, Charles. You go ahead," she said, waving him off. She was a woman used to being obeyed. Charlie nodded and walked out, pointedly motioning Calderon ahead of him. Ross the surfer came in a moment later, carrying a whiskey sour in a tulip glass on a small silver tray.

"Thank you, dear," she said, taking the glass, sipping the liquor greedily. "Now, would you please bring one of the cars around and wait out front? Miss Mitchell will need a lift into town shortly."

Ross glanced at me, then nodded and stalked off, closing the door after him.

"I knew your father," she said, swiveling her chair to face me, cocking her head with that kittenish tilt to look me over. "You favor him a bit, tall and dark. Much prettier, of course, though he was no slouch in that department. Before my accident, I used to sail a lot. I bought equipment from him and he gave me a few pointers. Unfortunately, he never did get around to giving me the sort of pointers he gave so many other girls. Pity."

Surprise must have shown in my face.

"Oh, don't look so shocked. At my age, I only regret the fun things I missed doing. Like getting pointers from your father. I understand you inherited his business. Are you working with the sheriff's department, as well?"

"No, I just do occasional diving jobs for Charlie."

"Good, then there'll be no conflict of interest if I hire you to do a small job for me."

"What kind of a job?"

"Suppose we call it . . . baby-sitting, of a sort. Mr. Calderon is upset and I expect he's going to be making some inquiries. As an outsider, he won't know whom to ask, or what to ask, and

31

he's liable to blunder around . . . upsetting people. Frankly, I'd like to minimize any fuss, for my son's sake. I sympathize with Mr. Calderon, of course, but I have my own family to think of. So, I'd like you to do what you can to help him, but also try to see that he's as . . . discreet as possible. You understand, I'm sure."

"I think so," I said. "You want to pay me to keep Calderon discreet. And I take it I'm supposed to be discreet, too?"

She hesitated, eyeing me with frank curiosity. "Something like that," she said, nodding.

"Actually," I said, "I think I can save you some money, Mrs. McClain. I'll help Calderon as a simple courtesy. As you said, none of this is his fault. And you needn't worry about me carrying tales about what was said here tonight, because, as far as I'm concerned, it's no one else's business, including mine. What's more, it won't cost you a dime."

"My, my," she said slowly, with a mischievous grin. "I believe I've pushed one of your hot buttons, as the kids say. I meant no offense, Miss Mitchell."

"None taken," I said. "Was there anything else?"

"Yes. Please come and see me again sometime, just to talk. The only visitors I get nowadays are old friends, and I mean *old* friends, or people with their hands out. I could use a new friend."

"Can't we all," I said.

7
ROSS

"SHE'S AT least half-crazy, you know," Ross said. We were in a Lincoln Town Car, gliding silently along the lakeshore drive. I looked him over as he spoke. Up close, I revised my first impression of him. He was older than I'd thought, late forties, maybe even more. His dark hair had the faint plum highlights of a rinse, and the skin around his eyes was a tad too taut across his cheekbones to be natural. Cosmetic surgery? He'd be the type, I suppose.

It must be pretty grim to be a paid companion and suddenly start noticing crow's-feet and gray hairs. Come to think of it, it's not much fun no matter what business you're in. Even mine.

"She was sharp tonight, on top of things," he continued, keeping his eyes on the road. "But on her bad days, she can be a handful. Did she want to hire you for something or other?"

I glanced at him without answering.

"I'm just trying to do my job, lady," he said, giving me a flash of too-perfect teeth in a practiced, professional grin. "Sometimes it includes being nosy."

"And what is your job, exactly?"

"Rent-a-pal," he said frankly. "I help her in and out of her chair, fetch and carry, cook for her sometimes, cheer her up when she's down, and generally try to keep her out of trouble."

"What kind of trouble would that be?"

"Oh, you'd be surprised. For instance, on her bad days, she watches those TV shopping shows and orders things over the phone, everything from mink coats to phony gold stocks, and then she forgets about it. Until they show up and the bills come in. She gets agitated sometimes and wants to drive alone and I have to jolly her out of it before she kills somebody."

"She can drive?"

"Sure. She's got a little modified minivan. It's minus a driver's seat so she can control it from her chair. On the days when she's got things together, she can handle it pretty well. Carts herself all over the place. But on her bad days . . ."

"Why are you telling me this?"

"Miss, I'm just trying to avoid problems. Audrey gets enthusiastic about things, about shopping, or going visiting. Whatever. But when she forgets about them, and if something crops up to remind her . . . well, I just hate to see her unhappy, you know? I think this Calderon business last week upset her more than she's letting on. It'd be better if he didn't come around again. A lot better."

"Better for whom?" I asked.

"For Audrey. I really do like her, you know. When she's up, she can be a real trip to be around. But just so we understand each other, if she's hired you for anything, you'd better clear it with Owney or me if you expect to get paid. Next time you see Audrey, she may not remember who you are. Maybe she won't even remember who she is."

"I see," I said, considering it.

"So, did she offer you some kind of a job?" he asked.

"Is Ross your first name or your last?" I asked.

He glanced at me a moment, reading my eyes. "Whichever," he said, with a vacant smile. "I'm just Ross."

8

PLANNING THE HUNT

CHARLIE BAUER'S county Blazer was parked in the Crow's Nest lot when Ross dropped me off. Charlie and Ray Calderon were alone at a corner table. Charlie, bear-sized in his brown uniform jacket, was stolidly munching one of Red's cheeseburger deluxes, a two-fisted dinner even with paws the size of Charlie's. Calderon was sipping a straight whiskey, not his first, judging from the flush of his jaw. Maybe serious drinking ran in the family.

"Hi," I said, easing down across from Charlie. "Any news?"

"Mr. Calderon here made a call, but nobody back home has heard anything from his brother, so I contacted the Coast Guard. We'll start an air search of the lake tomorrow. How much area do you figure we should cover?"

"That's hard to say," I said, hesitant to speak openly with Calderon there.

"It's all right," Ray said, as though he'd read my mind. "I know the drill. How far could a body drift in a week?"

"Well, as I mentioned, the river current's thrust is still palpable a mile or more from the mouth," I explained. "It might even be as far as two miles, with all the rain we've had. Deep water's temperature's roughly forty degrees, so bodies rise fairly quickly, say within twenty-four to forty-eight hours tops. The prevailing wind's been from the northeast the past week, so the floater—excuse me, the body—would drift south once it surfaced. I doubt it could be more than five miles out, so an air search in an eight-mile arc from the river mouth would give us a three-mile margin for error. Plus, you should probably do a ground search along the South Point shoreline."

"You're assuming the torso's intact," Calderon said quietly. "If it's been punctured, the body may already have sunk. What about scavengers? Gulls or fish?"

"The Great Lakes don't have any scavenger fish that work on the surface, at least no large ones. Gulls might attack a fl—"

"Go ahead and call it a floater," Calderon snapped. "I'm familiar with the term."

"Sorry, I'm just trying to . . . In any case, your brother was wearing a leather jacket when I saw him. It wasn't in the car, so if he was wearing it when he went in, it would protect his upper body from gulls. I think there's a fair chance the body's still afloat, possibly already ashore."

"Wouldn't somebody have found it if it had washed up?"

"Maybe not," Charlie put in. "Tourist season's over, and a lot of the houses along South Point are summer homes."

"I see. And if the body's already sunk?"

I glanced at Charlie, not wanting to say it.

"If that's the case, then I'm afraid the chances for a recovery drop off pretty sharply," Charlie said calmly. "In the spring when the ice breaks up, it might be carried ashore. But to be absolutely frank with you, Mr. Calderon, if we don't recover the body in the next few days, it's quite possible we may never find it. Of course, it's also possible it isn't in the lake at all."

"How do you mean?"

"Well, so far we've been assuming the worst. We find the car in the river, suitcases in the trunk. Granted, it looks bad. But suppose your brother made it out of the car okay? He'd been drinking, and he'd just had a big disappointment. In effect, he'd

36

lost his father for the second time. It's just possible he decided to hell with it all and took off. Young guys do that sometimes. I even did it once myself."

"No," Calderon said softly. "I don't think he . . . ran off. I think Jimmy's dead. I'm almost certain of it."

"Why do you say that?" Charlie asked.

"I know it here," Calderon said, tapping his heart. "I've felt it for days. We were very close as kids. My mom remarried a few years after Jimmy was born. A sailor. So we grew up as navy brats, always on the move, different bases, different schools almost every year. All we had was each other. Then I went into the service myself and Jimmy . . . Excuse me, I think I'd better take a walk," he said, rising abruptly, his eyes misty. "Is there a motel around here?"

"A couple," Charlie said. "Harbor Inn's the best, half mile or so down the shore. I'll be glad to drop you."

"No, I'll find it. You finish your dinner. There is one thing, though. The air search? I'd like to go along. I'm not an amateur. I won't get in the way."

"I can ask," Charlie said. "Can't guarantee anything. It'll be up to the Coast Guard pilot."

"Thanks," Calderon said. "For everything. You, too, ma'am. And I'm sorry if I've seemed rude."

"No problem," I said. "I'm just sorry things . . . haven't turned out better for you."

"Right. I'll be at that motel if anything . . . well, you know." He turned and walked out without a backward glance. And I'm human. I couldn't help noticing how well he carried himself, even though he had to be hurting. The way his shoulders moved . . . Charlie was watching me.

"So," I said, reaching across and stealing one of his french fries. "Do you think he's right? The feeling he's got about his brother, I mean?"

"Hard to say," Charlie said. "I've never experienced it my-self, but I've run into it a few times over the years. People call

37

the station and ask us to check on somebody, usually a parent, because they've had a bad dream or maybe just a strong feeling something bad's happened to the person."

"And?" I prompted. "How does it turn out?"

"It's only come up a few times," Charlie said with a shrug. "It's not like I've done a big scientific study or anything."

"And you're ducking the question. Are they ever right or not?"

"They're always right," he said sourly, pushing his plate aside. "Every goddamned time."

9

THE HUNT

RAY CALDERON went up with the Coast Guard chopper the next day. For nearly ten hours, they crisscrossed an imaginary grid over roughly eighty square miles of open water. The weather was ideal for a search, a brassy, beautiful October day, light wind, waves less than a foot high, visibility damned near unlimited. Late that afternoon, Charlie buzzed me to tell me they'd struck out completely, both in the air and the ground search along the shore. But when Calderon wandered into the Nest a little after seven that night, there was no disappointment in his face, nor much of anything else. He was a closed book to me. But one I thought might be interesting to read.

He was dressed semiformally for this part of the country—jeans, with a jacket and tie. He took the same corner table he and Charlie had shared the night before, and I wandered over.

"Hi," I said. "Charlie told me how the search went. I'm sorry."

"Maybe no news is good news." He shrugged. "Can I buy you a drink?"

"No thanks," I said, sitting down across the table from him. "But I'm a pretty good listener."

"I don't need a shoulder to cry on," he said. "Not yet, anyway. I could use a little professional advice, though, if you wouldn't mind?"

· "Not at all. How can I help?"

"The Coast Guard pilot told me that this time of year, with the weather and water temperature as cool as they are, a floater will stay on the surface for quite a while. Sometimes for weeks."

"It's possible." I nodded.

"Well, we covered roughly a six-mile arc today, which is the largest part of the projected search area, and you couldn't ask for a clearer look than we had up there. We'll take another crack at it tomorrow, but at this point it's a pretty good bet that either the body's already gone down . . . or, just maybe, Bauer was right. Maybe it's somewhere else."

"How do you mean?"

"Well, we don't know for a fact that my brother was in the car when it went in. The sheriff said there was no blood or interior damage to indicate he was injured. Maybe there's some other explanation."

"You mean that maybe he took off after all?"

"No. I wish I could believe that, but I just can't make it add up. Are you a gambler, Miss Mitchell?"

"Call me Mitch," I said. "And I've been known to drop a few bucks at poker. Why?"

"Then you know a little about probabilities. About odds. My little brother comes to a town he's never been in before, doesn't know a soul here. He makes some inquiries about a guy who supposedly died umpty years ago but who also happens to be a wanted felon. And then, poof, he disappears," he said, snapping his fingers. "He's gone, just like that. What do you figure the odds are that it's a coincidence?"

"I couldn't say," I said carefully. "But that may be exactly what it is."

"An accident?" he said. "Okay, it was an accident. So where's the body?"

"Mr. Calderon, people do disappear in the big lake. Last year,

40

someone . . . very close to me went through the ice. We never found him."

"But they usually do turn up, right? More often than not?"

"More often than not, yes."

"Then all I'm saying is, for Jimmy to die accidentally only a few hours after he arrived, and for his body to disappear, too, strikes me as one heckuva long shot."

"Long shots do come in sometimes."

"You're right," he agreed. "Sometimes you fill an inside straight and sometimes the turtle beats the rabbit. But betting long shots is no way to save for your old age, is it? Besides, I've been thinking about what Mrs. McClain told us last night. She lied to us until I called her on it, you know. And now I wonder how much of the rest of it was true."

"The rest of what?"

"I don't know," he said, exasperated. "I'm not saying she's an archcriminal or anything, but her health's obviously pretty shaky. Maybe her memory is, too. Maybe she forgot something."

"Ross, her butler, or whatever he is, says she has good and bad days," I conceded. "He also suggested strongly that we stay away from her. And maybe he's right. She seems in rough shape."

"No argument there, but what about the other lady who was there? The one she said stopped by?"

"Megan Lundy?"

"Right. Do you know her?"

"To say hello to. She's an artist, teaches at the local community college."

"I'd really like to talk to her, just on the off chance that she can help. But since she doesn't know me from Adam, I wonder, could you give her a call for me and arrange some kind of a meeting?"

"I can try. I'll even come along, if you like."

"I'd appreciate that a lot. It might make things easier."

"Not at all. But just so we understand each other, Mr. Calderon—"

"Mr. Calderon's my dad. Or he was. Call me Ray, please."

"Okay, Ray, then. The thing is, Mrs. McClain offered to pay me to be your . . . chaperone, I suppose. She's afraid you might embarrass her family."

"I've got nothing against them. Hell, I suppose in an odd way we're related. So how much is she paying you?"

"Nothing. I turned her down."

"You turned her down? Then why are you helping me?"

"I turned down the money," I said. "I didn't say I didn't want the job."

10
WOMYN IN CHAINS

MEGAN LUNDY'S home was only a mile or so up the Lake Huron shore from the McClains'. It was a converted summer retreat, a pleasantly weathered two-story driftwood gray clapboard salt-box with chocolate eaves and shutters. It was flanked by eyeless vacation cabins, closed for the season, from the look of them.

I rang the buzzer and a voice from above yelled at us to come around back.

A broad redwood deck with balustered railings had been built out from the rear of the house at the second-story level to overlook the rocky beach and the bay. We climbed an ornate spiral stairway up to the deck. And stepped into Wonderland.

A barefoot young woman with stringy auburn hair was dully stirring an empty pot on a prop kitchen stove at the far corner of the deck. Her threadbare plaid flannel bathrobe was open to the waist, revealing her breasts and the silky curve of her abdomen. She was in her mid-twenties, and five or six months pregnant. And she was in chains.

Black iron manacles encircled her wrists and a heavy chain draped from them to the deck. She glanced up sharply as Ray stepped onto the deck. She eyed us with mild curiosity for a moment, but then her thoughts seemed to turn inward again, and she returned to her pseudo labor.

Megan Lundy was lost in her work, thrusting with her brush like a duelist at a three-by-four-foot canvas held on an easel. Megan was a big-boned woman, wearing a paint-spattered faded blue terry-cloth jumpsuit. She was in her late forties, with a squarish face, broad shoulders, a wide bottom, and no discernible waistline between. Her face was handsome rather than pretty, with heavy brows that matched her close-cropped salt-and-pepper hair. Her intense dark eyes gave it a special life.

"Hi, make yourselves at home," she said absently. "I'll be done in a few minutes. Hate to lose the light. October light is . . ." Her voice trailed off as her consciousness disappeared into her art.

Ray strolled to the railing, politely giving his back to the half-dressed girl. He folded his arms and stared out over the water, and I sensed a "Do Not Disturb" sign in his stance.

A pair of French doors opened into a studio and I wandered in. It was a huge room for the size of the house. All the inner partitions had been removed, leaving naked steel jack posts to support the roof. The wall facing the lake and the two adjoining were mostly glass, huge picture windows with an incredible view of the sky and the shore. The streetside wall was covered with paintings. Some were properly hung, but many more were just stacked one atop the other.

Most of the subjects were similar to the scene on the deck, women of various ages, physiques, and races, some pregnant, some not. They were all shown at tasks—typing, washing their hair, mopping a floor, bathing a child. And all were in shackles, though some of the chains were laced with flowers, and a few gleamed like precious metal. Some of the figures were making love. No. Not love. They were having sex. But there was nothing erotic about it. The women were beautifully rendered, nude, suppliant. The men were less clearly drawn. Their faces were vague and they were all shown fully clothed, in business suits, or dungarees. One was even holding a briefcase while he

44

entered his manacled nude partner anally as she leaned over a crib, cooing to her child. The colors were subtle, pastels that might be found on any motel wall, an artistic understatement that gave the work an even fiercer impact.

And the paintings *were* powerful, seething with passion that would have set a stone ablaze. But there were too many. My eyes were drawn from one to the next so quickly, I had to turn away to keep from being overwhelmed.

The window ledges were cluttered with half-squeezed tubes of paint, discarded pencils, charcoal stubs. And handcuffs and shackles. I picked a pair up, wondering if they were props. Nope. They were very real indeed. Odd. The shackles probably weighed no more than a pound or two each, yet the bondage they represented made them seem infinitely heavier.

A small table draped in midnight blue velvet stood in one corner, a display of a different kind. They were ceramic replicas of what appeared to be primeval figures, rude clay earth mothers with swollen bellies and breasts. One of them was so striking, I actually caught my breath: a pregnant nude goddess, rising from water, her arms raised in victory. She looked ancient and familiar at the same time, as though I'd worshiped her in another life. I was utterly enchanted. Without thinking, I reached out for her.

"Please don't touch them, Mitch," Megan Lundy said. "Some of them were never fired, so they're quite fragile. She's from my Ashtoreth period."

"Ashtoreth?" I said, glancing up. On the deck, the model was pulling a pair of slacks on under her bathrobe. Ray was still at the rail, watching the last of the light fade into the water.

"Ashtoreth, the Phoenician goddess of fertility," Megan said, tossing a gauze dustcover over the display. "I'll bet I did a hundred different versions of her in college. And sold about two. I keep these around to remind me that there's more to art than passion."

"They're very powerful," I said. "The figure rising from water . . ."

45

"That's right, you're the diver, aren't you? Must be a tough field for a woman to break into," she said briskly, taking my arm and leading me to the wall of art. "And what do you make of my current endeavors?"

"They're stunning," I said honestly. "They're almost too much to absorb at once."

"I'm outta here, Meg," the model said, popping her head in the door. "Think you'll stop over later?"

"I'll call you," Megan said, giving the girl a good-bye kiss that lingered a heartbeat too long to be sisterly. The girl whispered something to Megan, then waved good-bye in my general direction and wandered off.

"Oh, to be that young again." Megan sighed. "You were saying about the paintings?"

"I really like this series. They're rude and refined at the same time, and for somebody who says she gave up on passion, these canvases fairly bleed it."

"I didn't say I lost any passion," Megan said. "I just learned successful art requires more than youthful enthusiasm. I call this grouping *Womyn in Chains*—womyn, spelled with a y. Personally, I think they're a shade too topical for pure art, but they sell like proverbial hotcakes in New York. I earn more for turning over a couple of canvases now than for a semester of teaching."

"In that case, shouldn't you take some steps against breakins?" Calderon asked, joining us. "I mean, this place is all glass, and I didn't notice an alarm system anywhere."

"You're obviously an out-of-towner," Megan said dryly. "Nobody would steal art in Huron Harbor. I'd be lucky to get ten bucks a pop for these at the county fair. But in a chic gallery in the Apple, with suitable framing . . . You're smiling. Do you find my work amusing?"

"Of course," Calderon said, glancing at her. "It's meant to be ironic, isn't it?"

"In what way?"

"The chains," he said. "They're not attached to anything."

"You're exactly right," Megan said, nodding in approval. "It never ceases to amaze me how many supposedly knowledgeable, politically correct types who babble on about the meaning of my work miss that aspect of it completely. The truth is, the chains we forge for ourselves are much heavier than any shackles society puts on us. Or at least it's my truth."

"It is true, I think," Ray said, "but not only for women."

"No, of course not. We all shackle ourselves one way or another. You're very perceptive. I take it you're the Mr. Calderon Mitch phoned me about. Forgive me for rattling on. I know you didn't come to talk about art. How can I help you?"

"Mrs. McClain said you stopped by her home last week while my brother was visiting her. I was hoping you could tell me something that . . . well, that might help."

"I heard they found his car," she said. "I'm very sorry. He seemed like a nice young man; but I don't see how I can help you. He left a few minutes after I arrived."

"Mrs. McClain said they'd been drinking," I prompted.

"Yes, I think they'd both had a few, but . . . Look, I thought about what I was going to say after you called, Mitch. I meant to be tactful, but I've got no talent for it. And considering what's happened, maybe the truth flat out is better. And the truth is, your brother had a pretty fair buzz going when I got there, Mr. Calderon. He was flushed, he was angry, and he was more than a little belligerent. In fact, I asked him to leave."

"You asked him to leave? Why?" Ray asked.

"He was out of line," Megan said bluntly. "He was rambling on about how he'd been cheated all his life, and part of *this*— which I took to mean Audrey's home and whatever—should have been his. Audrey was visibly upset and . . . anyway, I asked him to go, and he did."

"How drunk would you say he was? Too drunk to drive?"

"I wouldn't think so," Megan said, frowning. "I mean, he wasn't staggering or anything. But since I don't drive myself, it's hard for me to judge."

"You don't drive?"

"I'm a transplanted New Yorker. I attended college here as

47

a girl, then came back to live and to teach a dozen years or so ago. The town's small enough that I can ride my bike or walk most places. I was jogging that day. In any case, your brother stormed out, and that's really all I can tell you. I'm sorry. This must be awful for you. I wish I could be of more help."

"Perhaps you can. Tell me, did you know Mrs. McClain's husband, Owen?"

"Owen?" Megan said, surprised. "Not really. I met him once or twice when I was in school."

"You were in school together?"

"No, he was a few years older, but Audrey was quite active in the arts when I was an undergrad, so I knew her. They came to fund-raisers and things together. God, they were a gorgeous couple in those days. Life can be . . . well, you know."

"Actually I don't. What happened to them?"

"Owen died in Vietnam and Audrey had a fall. Lost her baby and the use of her legs. Lost everything, really."

"Take a look at this," he said, handing her the photograph. "Would you say this is a good likeness of Mr. McClain?"

"Doesn't do him justice." She grimaced. "He was quite a hunk back then, as I recall."

"And now?" Calderon said. "What would he look like now?"

"Now?" she echoed, puzzled. "What do you mean?"

"The FBI has computers that can age a person's photograph. You're an artist, a very good one. Do you think you could sketch a likeness of Owen the way he might look today?"

"You want a sketch of Owen?" she said. "What on earth for? I don't understand."

"I'm not sure I do, either. But my brother came to this town, looking for a man, and a few hours later he disappeared. Maybe it was an accident. But if it wasn't, I can only think of one person who'd have a reason to harm him."

"You mean Owen? But he's dead."

"So people keep telling me," Calderon said mildly. "But since no one seems to be sure exactly how he died, or where he's buried, I'd say there's at least an outside chance that . . . rumors of his death have been exaggerated."

"Look, I'm very sorry for your trouble," Megan said evenly, "but I couldn't do what you ask, even if I thought you might be right. Audrey McClain is an old friend who's had more than her share of pain in her life. I wouldn't risk hurting her for the world. I'm sorry."

"You needn't be," Calderon said. "I understand. Thank you for seeing me. And I really do like your work very much. If you think of anything that might help, I'm staying at the Harbor Inn." He took the photo from her and walked across the deck and down the stairway.

"What an intriguing guy," Megan said thoughtfully. "Have you known him long?"

"No, ma'am," I said. "I scarcely know him at all."

11
AROUND THE BEND

"Do you have any idea how crazy that sounded?" I asked. We were in my Jeep, headed back to the Nest.

"Maybe it does," he said quietly. "But the idea kept eating at me in the chopper today, looking down at all that empty water. There's nothing complicated about it. If Jimmy went into the river, then he should still be in the water somewhere, and that lake was laid out like a giant copper mirror, scarcely a ripple on it. If he was down there, we should have spotted him. Working air/sea rescue, I've found people in the Atlantic in rough weather with visibility less than a hundred yards. It just didn't figure that we couldn't find Jimmy somehow. If he was there to be found."

"But you don't think he is?"

"I honestly don't know," he said somberly. "I wish I did, but I don't. But here's the thing: If he didn't die in that river, if he wasn't in that car, then whatever happened to him probably wasn't an accident at all. Does that sound like a reasonable assumption?"

"As far as it goes, I suppose it does," I admitted.

"And if it wasn't an accident, then a couple of other questions pop up. Who would have reason to harm him, and how could it happen so quickly? And the only answer I could come up with is Owen McClain."

"But Mrs. McClain said he never came back here. They even had him declared dead."

"Well, for openers, he wouldn't have come back here right away, not with the army looking for him. But let's say he showed up a few years later. Do you really think his family would just turn him in to the army to do a long stretch in Leavenworth for attempted murder and desertion? Or would they figure he'd suffered enough and help him start over? Maybe buy him a new identity, possibly even a new face with cosmetic surgery? From the looks of that house, I'd say they can probably afford to do anything that needed doing."

"But if he's still wanted by the military, why would he risk staying here? He could be anywhere."

"No, I think he'd be nearby. His people are here; his money's here. But most of all, I think he's here because my brother fell off the world the day he showed up looking for him."

"I see," I said slowly. "What are you going to do?"

"In the morning, I'm going out with the Coast Guard again for another air search over the lake. If we come up empty, they'll have done all they can and they'll pack it in."

"But you won't?"

"No, ma'am, I'll just be getting started. Look, I can't just walk away from this. I can't go home without my brother. He was all I had, and I was all he had. And if I'd looked out for him a little better, the way brothers are supposed to, maybe he wouldn't have come here at all."

"You can't be sure of that. He might well have come anyway."

"Yeah, maybe so. And it wasn't like I'd given up on him or anything. Hell, it's already cost me . . . Well, it doesn't matter. None of it matters now."

"Cost you what? What were you going to say?"

"Nothing, I was just feeling sorry for myself. Whatever it's cost me is nothing compared to what it cost him. The bottom

51

line is, there's no way I can just . . . abandon him here. Surely you can understand that?"

"I don't know," I said honestly. "I think it depends on whether you're staying to look for your brother, or Owen McClain."

"Maybe if I find the one, I'll find the other. My brother's the reason I came. But I may ask around about the possibly not-so-late Mr. McClain while I'm at it. He won't mind. Not if he's really dead, right?"

"His family might mind, though. You'll be dredging up a lot of unhappiness I'm sure they'd rather forget."

"I'm sorry about that, but I don't see what I can do about it. All I want is the truth. And sometimes the truth hurts."

"You're the one it could hurt, Ray. Huron Harbor's a small town. The McClains have a lot of friends and a fair amount of clout here."

"How much clout? Do they own Sheriff Bauer, for instance?"

"No, nobody owns Charlie. But let's say you're right and Owen is here, which I don't believe for a second. If you start asking a lot of questions, won't you just scare him off?"

"He didn't run when my brother asked about him. He took him out. But Jimmy was really just a kid. I haven't been a kid for a long, long time."

"I see," I said slowly, and I really did. "You think if he's here, he may try to kill you, don't you? And you want him to."

He looked over at me a moment, with eyes as empty as an Aztec mask. He didn't answer me. He didn't have to.

12

RUNNING FOR COVER

"I FIGURE nuclear war will be next," I said. "Or maybe the black plague."

"Who's gonna get nuked?" Red said. "Anybody I know?"

"Sure; me. Troubles are supposed to come in threes, and right now I'd be happy to swap the baker's dozen I seem to have for any three you could name." We were running on the beach along the Lake Huron shore south of the Nest. Correction: I was running, working at it, panting, sweating through my faded MSU sweatshirt and cutoffs. Red was loping along in a long-legged groove that barely raised a dew on her forehead. Gulls wheeled overhead in a copper October sky, reflected on the mirrored surface of the big lake with only the tidal ripples to mar their image. A perfect day for a run. And for an air search.

I could hear the distant drone of a light plane over the horizon, but maybe it was just an echo in my imagination.

"How much trouble are you really in?" Red asked. "Financially, I mean."

"A lot. I need to come up with some serious cash to repair the Nest, and I not only don't have it, I haven't a glimmer of an idea about how to get it. Without the repairs, we probably won't pass our next city inspection, and if they close us down, I'll have to sell out. No choice."

"You don't want to sell. You might actually have to go back to working for a living. You said a baker's dozen. What else is wrong?"

"This business with Calderon. I feel awful about what happened to his brother, whatever it was, and I'd like to help if I can, but I've also got troubles of my own. Maybe it's small-minded of me, but his timing could have better."

"So there goes your shot at the Humanitarian of the Year award. But while we're being cold and calculating about it, unfortunate as the situation is, if you backed away from it, you probably wouldn't be stoned in the village square. Some folks might even give you a medal."

"A medal? Why?"

"I've been hearing some rumblings, nothing specific, just bits and pieces of conversations while I'm working. Some of the shop rats that work at the McClain fuels plant have the idea that Calderon means trouble for them."

"What kind of trouble?"

"I don't know. I doubt that they do, either. It's just a rumor—you know how it goes. To be honest, I didn't pay much attention to it."

"Maybe you should have."

"Why? Look, the bottom line is: Calderon may be a nice guy, and I'm sorry he's jammed up, but ain't we all, one way and another? His problems aren't yours, Mitch. He's a big boy. He can take care of himself."

I mulled over what she said as I ran. She was right, of course. My first loyalty was to my son and myself, and right now I didn't have much room to maneuver. I'd worked too hard to set the Nest to rights to give it up without a fight. Still, I had to admit, there was something about Ray that moved me in a way I hadn't felt for a very long time. . . . Red was staring at me oddly. "What?" I asked.

"You're a thousand miles away, girlfriend. Maybe this

54

Calderon is a bigger boy than I thought. Are you interested?"

"In what?"

"In Calderon? Come on, just between us."

"Get serious. I barely know him."

"Sometimes barely is the best way. He's not my type, of course—wrong gender—but as a neutral observer, I'd say he qualifies for hunkdom. If you like the rugged Latin type. And who doesn't?"

"That's crap and you know it."

"Right," she agreed dryly. "Sure it is. Okay, back to problem one. The money. What are you going to do?"

"For openers, I'm going to take inventory," I said grimly, picking up my pace. "It's time to do it anyway, and however things come out, I'd better have a rough idea of what the stock is worth."

13

TAKING STOCK

THAT AFTERNOON I did my best to put banks, roof beams, collateral, and Ray Calderon out of my mind. I left Red and the cook on their own in the Nest, locked myself in the dive shop, and began the postsummer inventory. Masks, snorkels, Hyperthane fins, Rapala lures—every display had to be checked against the stock lists. The diving season was over, but the hunting season was already on us, and soon I'd need to spend most of my time in the bar/restaurant half of the Nest.

I suppose taking inventory should be considered scut work, but the truth is, I love doing it, love being alone in my own shop with the sweet oily scent of new gear and the bright gumdrop colors of Hyperthane fins and snorkels. I grew up in this shop, and some of the happiest times of my childhood were here. So I time-traveled as I worked, spending a few hours with the girl I'd once been, remembering her dreams, and some of her fears, and occasionally glimpsing the person I've become through her eyes. We get along quite well, that girl and I, despite the difference in our ages.

But we weren't alone. Images of Ray and his brother kept intruding at odd moments. I grew up without siblings. My mother died having me, and my father's mom took me and raised me as her own until I was twelve. When Alzheimer's took her away into its shadowy ghost world of lost memories, I came north to live with my father, a man I barely knew, and one whose parenting skills might have been adequate for raising a pack of wolves. Still, he tried. He taught me his trade: diving, and about boats, and even guns. I'm sure any Psych 101 student would offer up an instant analysis that my father secretly wanted a son. Wrong. I doubt he wanted any kids at all. Granted, he was no paragon of parenthood. Who is? I think he did the best he could. He taught me what he knew. He tried to ready me for the world, and I did learn a lot from him about life. Although, to be honest, most of what I gleaned from his example was how not to live it.

The summer I graduated from high school, I had a lot too much to drink at a party, and I passed out. I'm not clear on what happened next. The term they use for it now is *date rape*. At the time, it was a disaster, the end of my life as I knew it. I was pregnant, couldn't bring myself to have the abortion my father insisted on, and so I ran away.

And found my life. When my son, Corey, was born, I was young, single, and very much on my own. I scuffled at first, supporting us with odd jobs, and eventually found work as a maintenance diver on the oil platforms in the Texas Gulf. I had no option but to place Corey in a private school, but he seemed to like it well enough. After spending the summer here with me, Corey asked if he could return to Texas to finish middle school with his friends. One more year. It hurt, but I agreed. A year. Every week without him seemed like a year to me now. And he'd only been gone a month. And six days. And fourteen hours.

Being away from Corey is an agony for me. But at least when we part, I know I'll see him again soon. I could only imagine what Jimmy's death meant to Ray, and yet his pain seemed so real to me that it might have been my own.

Was it just sympathy? Or were we connecting on a deeper, more intense level? Red was absolutely right. I definitely found him attractive, and unless my emotional radar was completely on the blink, I could sense the same feelings in him. But at this point in my life . . .

A knock on the shop door snapped me out of it. I considered not answering, but whoever was knocking could read the CLOSED sign. Ray? I opened it cautiously.

"Hi," Megan Lundy panted, "got a minute?" Her face was flushed, gleaming with perspiration. She'd obviously been working hard at something and she was dressed for it, in a faded mauve sweat suit and scuffed high-mileage Nikes.

"Come on in," I said. "Did you jog all the way over from your studio?"

"Nope, I rode in style. Mountain bike. But I did a color tour of the hills west of town first, trying to decide whether I should come here at all."

"Well, I'm glad you made it. Can I get you a drink? Water? Gatorade? Whatever?"

"No thanks," she said, glancing around the shop curiously. "Actually, I wanted to talk to you about your friend Calderon. Are we alone?"

"Just us and the ghosts of summer," I said. "What about Ray?"

"He's been making me crazy, that's what about him. That little speech he made last night about Owen McClain, and what he might look like now? Mind you, I don't think he's right, but . . . I just couldn't get the idea out of my head. So I did a few sketches, just variations of the picture he showed me." She took a sketch pad out of her jacket and handed it to me, but she held my hand closed on it.

"I want your promise to be careful with this," she said. "I'm willing to help, as much to satisfy my own curiosity as anything, but I wouldn't want to hurt Audrey McClain in any way, or even have her think I was being disloyal."

"Keeping Ray Calderon discreet is becoming a second career for me lately," I said, opening the book. The first two drawings showed Owen with various beards. The third made me pause.

"That one's Owen plus a couple of metric tons," she explained, watching my face.

"He . . . seems familiar," I said.

"Yes, I noticed it, too," she said. "He looks a bit like Owney's uncle Gordon. Probably just a family resemblance. Blubber tends to blur lines of distinction."

"Too true," I said, flipping through the others. They showed Owen bald, partially bald, and . . . with a bushy mane of hair and a seamed face. "This one could almost be Ross."

"It could also be David Bowie on a bad-hair day," Megan said wryly. "That's the problem. Once you start wondering about a thing like this, you start to see Owen's ghost everywhere. I imagine that's how conspiracy cults get started."

"What's this one?" I asked. It was a cartoon sketch of a crone, at least eighty.

"A cautionary reminder."

"Of what? It's an old woman."

"Look again. For a young woman."

"Ah," I said, nodding, "right. I see her." The two faces shared the same lines, but the women depicted were decades apart, facing in different directions.

"It's a child's game, but it might be a good thing for Ray to keep in mind. These are just sketches. They don't prove anything, and by the way, I'm doing them as much for you as for your friend."

"For me?"

"I enjoyed talking to you last night. You struck me as an interesting character. I love this town and the lake country, but sometimes, as a professional woman on my own, I feel like what's-her-name in *The Clan of the Cave Bear*. Surrounded by strangers who don't quite speak the same language. Ever have that feeling?"

"Sometimes," I admitted. "Especially lately."

"My life's a shambles right now," Megan said briskly. "I'm having a solo show in New York at the end of the month and I still have several paintings to finish for it. But afterward? What do you say we get together for an evening sometime, just to get acquainted. A little white wine, a lot of girl talk. How does that sound?"

"It sounds terrific," I said honestly. "I'd like that very much. I really admire your work."

"I'd return the compliment," she said, glancing curiously around the shop, "if I had even the vaguest idea of what it is you do. But I look forward to hearing about it. When the first snow flies, say?" She offered me her hand. "Deal?"

"Deal," I agreed. "When the first snow flies."

14

THE ARRANGEMENT

⁓◦⁓

"INTERESTING," RAY said, flipping through the sketches that night. Dinner at the Nest was becoming a habit, or perhaps I just hoped it would be. He looked tired. He'd flown most of the day with the Coast Guard chopper. They'd had no luck at all. He paused a moment at the sketch that resembled Ross, then flipped past it. "Last night, she said she wouldn't help. Why do you suppose she changed her mind?"

"I don't know. She said she couldn't get the idea out of her head."

"I know the feeling," he said. "So. Other than the McClain's butler or whatever—what's his name, Ross?—does anyone else look familiar to you?"

"Sure. Unfortunately, too many of them do. There are twelve thousand people who live in this town, thirty thousand in the county. That may be small potatoes compared with Detroit or Norfolk, but it's still a lot of people. I don't know all of them, or even most of them."

"My mother said Jimmy was taller than his father but not as heavily built. That eliminates everybody who isn't roughly six foot, and, say, a hundred and seventy or eighty pounds minimum. Does that narrow it down any?"

The edge in Ray's voice made me hesitant to mention the overweight Owen's resemblance to Gordon McClain. Fortunately, Charlie Bauer interrupted us. He spotted us as soon as he stepped into the room, and he came directly over. He may have looked normal to Ray; his brown county uniform was slightly disheveled and his guileless face seemed as open as an apple pie. But something was up. I sensed it in the way he moved.

"Mitch, Mr. Calderon, mind if I join you?" He took the chair beside me without waiting for an answer. "I heard the air search came up empty again today, Mr. Calderon. I'm sorry."

"Me, too," Ray said. "The pilot was a good man, though. A stone pro. He did his best."

"And so did we," Charlie said. "My men extended their range today. We either checked with the owners or searched the beach ourselves for a full ten miles along the south shore. We found the wreck of a motorboat that was stolen a few weeks ago, but that was about it. There was no sign of your brother, and I'm afraid that's all we can do for the present. If there are any further developments, I'll contact you, of course. When will you be heading back to Norfolk?"

"Not right away. I think I may stay on for a while."

"I see. To look for your brother?"

"For that, and maybe more. Let me ask you something straight out, Charlie. That song and dance Mrs. McClain gave us about her husband being dead, legally and otherwise—did you buy it?"

"I think she believes it," Charlie said carefully. "Maybe she needs to. Which doesn't necessarily make it true. On the other hand, even if she's wrong and Owen is alive somewhere—which I seriously doubt—he's not around here."

"I understand there are thirty thousand people in this county. Do you know them all?"

"Nope, but I don't have to. I knew Owen. Played high school football with him, in fact. He was a few years older, but I knew him."

"And how long ago was that?"

"More years than I'd care to recall," Charlie said, unoffended. "But I'm fairly sure I'd still know him if I met him."

"Would *you*? How about these people?" he said, passing Charlie the sketch pad. "Do you know any of them?"

Charlie riffled through the pages, quickly at first, then again more slowly. He frowned at the cartoon of the old/young woman, then smiled. "Nice work. I'm impressed. Where'd you get these?"

"It doesn't matter. Do any of them look familiar?"

"Sure. All of them do. They're all Owen. The physical differences among them are general enough to resemble a fair number of folks."

"Good. So if I show them around enough, someone might recognize somebody eventually."

"Possibly. People still spot Elvis on a fairly regular basis. An identification from a sketch like this wouldn't prove doodley."

"I'm not interested in proving anything. But *if* he's here, I think there's a better than even chance he knows what happened to my brother. And if I find him, I think he'll tell me."

"I see. You know, Mr. Calderon, I lost a brother once, too. In Vietnam. I came back; he didn't. And it still hurts. And because of that, I'm not unsympathetic to your situation. But I can't have you crashin' around the countryside on some vigilante manhunt. Nothing'd come of it but trouble."

"I haven't broken any laws, Sheriff, but Owen McClain has. He's still wanted for attempted murder. The last guy we know of who crossed him ended up with a hole in his belly on a barracks room floor. And if he's managed to stay free all this time, I imagine he'd do whatever's necessary to keep it that way. Maybe even murder. So are you really worried about your constituents? Or could it be his family has a little too much . . . clout?"

Charlie eyed him for a moment without answering, but a rosy flush began to creep above his collar. "If Owen McClain was in my county, Mr. Calderon, I'd bust him like any other wanted felon, family or no, friendship or no. But I have no real reason to believe that he's actually here."

"No? You think my brother just happened to have a heck of a run of bad luck a few hours after he showed up looking for Owen?"

"No, sir, I didn't say that. I don't know what happened to your brother—yet. Neither do you. And I'm not ignoring the fact that he disappeared very soon after he arrived here, or that foul play might have been involved."

"No one here had a reason to harm him but Owen Mc-Clain."

"That's correct. No one *here*. But your brother was on parole, Mr. Calderon. Maybe some of his problems followed him here. Or some of yours did."

"Mine?"

"That's right, yours. I had a visitor waiting for me when I got back from searching the South Point shoreline this afternoon, Mr. Calderon. A navy CID officer—you know, from the Criminal Investigation Division? A Lieutenant Galloway. He says you two know each other pretty well. Is that right?"

Ray didn't respond. His face showed nothing at all.

"Mr. Calderon," Charlie said patiently, "I'm theoretically goin' out on a limb here, telling you about the lieutenant's visit. He asked me not to. A matter of national security, he said. So, since I'm risking the displeasure of the U.S. Navy, how about a civil answer to a simple question. Now, do you know this Lieutenant Galloway?"

Ray nodded. "I know him."

"That's better. I won't ask if you're friends; I take it you're not. In fact, the lieutenant seems to think you're a pretty unsavory character. Implied you might even be mixed up in the drug trade. He was a little vague about that part. What he wasn't vague about was that you constitute a definite threat to the peace and well-being of the good folks of Huron Harbor. He suggested in very strong terms that I ask you leave town. He all but ordered me to, in fact."

"I see. And are you going to try?"

"Try? Mr. Calderon, just so we understand each other, I may be a small-town sheriff, but if I ever decide I want you gone, I can damned sure figure a way to get it done."

"So why don't you?"

"Maybe I will. But if I do, it won't be because some shave-tail lieutenant blows a lotta smoke in my direction. I was a sergeant in Vietnam—Rangers. We followed orders more'n once that we knew were stupid. And I lost friends because of it. So nowadays, I'm kinda reluctant to take orders from people who are reluctant to explain 'em. You know what I mean?"

Ray nodded.

"Thought you might, you bein' ex-navy and all. So why don't you go a step further, maybe, and tell me what the hell's goin' on here."

"I'm sorry," Ray said, shaking his head slowly. "I'm afraid I can't do that. I truly can't."

"Straight enough." Charlie nodded. "I thought you might feel that way. So I took the liberty of doing a little checking up on my own, Mr. Calderon—nothing official, just a friendly phone call to my counterpart in Norfolk. He confirmed that Galloway is who he says he is, and he also knows who you are. And his opinion of you isn't much different from Galloway's. *Colorful.* That was the word he used. Said you got busted out of the navy under shady circumstances and you'd been running with some rough people since. Some of the same people your brother was mixed up with."

"We have some of the same friends," Calderon conceded. "Which is why I'm sure my brother's disappearance isn't con-nected to anything back home."

"But it could be," Charlie said. "And from where I'm sitting, it's a helluva lot more likely than Owen McClain hiding out up here under my nose. So I'll tell you what, Mr. Calderon. We're gonna do a deal, you and me. I'll take these sketches of yours, and I'll run a quiet background check on anyone who even vaguely matches up with 'em. I'll check work records, driver's licenses. I'll even run a fingerprint check if anything seems the slightest bit outta line. And if I turn up Owen McClain, I promise you I'll fall on him like a damned landslide. But if I come up empty, if they all check out clean, I want your word you'll go back to Norfolk and leave the McClain family alone. God knows, they've had enough grief because of Owen. They don't need any more."

"How do I know you'll actually investigate anything?"

"Because I just said so," Charlie said evenly. "If that's not good enough for you, that's too bad. It's the best deal you're gonna get."

Ray eyed him a moment, then nodded. "Fair enough. You take your best shot at this thing, and if you can't shake anything loose, I'll go."

"Good. I'll take your word for it—especially since I can make damn sure you keep it. I'll take the sketches and you take yourself a nice vacation. And I'd better not hear that you're harassing anyone. Clear?"

"I promise to stay out of your way," Ray said. "Good luck."

"I'll be in touch," Charlie said, rising. "Mitch, you take care." He hesitated, as if he wanted to say something more, then turned abruptly and made his way out through the dinner crowd.

"A very tactful guy," Calderon said, watching Charlie stalk off. "I think he wanted to warn you about me, but he didn't want to step over the line. Your line, not mine."

"Warn me about what? That you're a colorful character?"

"I plead guilty to being a character," he said. "But color's kind of in the eye of the beholder, don't you think?"

"What I think is, you gave up that sketchbook without much of an argument. I'm wondering why."

Calderon mulled the question a moment, then shrugged. "The bottom line is: I believed him when he said he wants to nail this bastard as much as I do. Plus, he knows the town and he can check out the people on that pad a lot more efficiently than I could."

"True," I said. "But there's more to it, isn't there? I can't see you sitting around waiting to see if Charlie turns anything up What are you going to do?"

"Since I'm technically on vacation, I think I'll take in some of the countryside."

"The countryside?"

"That's right. The way I figure it, if Jimmy's death wasn't accidental, then there may be a reason that his body hasn't turned up."

"How do you mean?"

"The way I read McClain, he's a rich, spoiled punk who turns violent when anyone crosses him. Let's say Jimmy caught up with him, or vice versa, sometime after he left the house. Maybe Owen followed him, or stopped him somewhere. They had words, and Owen . . . killed him. Now he's got a big problem. If the body turns up showing signs of violence, there's a damned short list of suspects. But if Jimmy's car is found in the river with no body in it, it's an accident. Case closed. So maybe we didn't find the body in the water because it was never there."

"And where do you think it is?"

"I was hoping you could help me with that. I'd guess it would have to be somewhere nearby. He didn't have time to plan anything complicated."

"Even so, there's a lot of open country around here, Ray. The state forest alone is thousands of acres."

"Is that where he'd go?"

"I don't know," I said slowly, considering the idea. "Maybe not. It's bow-hunting season. Bowmen hunt in all kinds of weather, and most of them are pretty fair trackers. I don't think he'd risk running into someone on open land or having a hunter stumble across the body. And he might not have to."

"Why not?"

"Because the McClain family owns quite a lot of property in the area, land he'd probably be familiar with."

"How much land?"

"A lot," I said. "If you hang on a moment, I can tell you exactly how much." I stepped into my office, rummaged through my desk, and came up with a county plat map pamphlet. I sat down beside Ray and flipped it open.

"These maps show property ownership for the county. According to this, the McClains own . . . wow, several thousand acres."

"Are you familiar with any of these places?"

"Some of them," I said. "This twelve-hundred-acre section here is the industrial fuels plant."

"That's where Jimmy went the first day, right?"

"Right. It's a big place, but it's fenced and well lighted and it's got security guards, plus it runs three shifts, twenty-four hours a day."

"It doesn't sound too likely, but maybe I should take a look at it. What is a fuels plant, anyway?"

"I'm not sure, exactly. I've never been inside the place. My understanding is that they convert trees and scrap wood from landfills into wood chips, then they truck the chips downstate for use as industrial fuel for power plants, things like that."

"How do they convert the trees into chips?"

"I don't know," I said slowly. "Grind them up somehow, I suppose."

"Whole trees? I imagine that'd take some pretty substantial machinery."

"Probably, but I really don't know. I do know a lot of people work there, though, around the clock. It's a busy place."

"Maybe I'll see just how busy it is sometime. But if there's a lot of activity, it doesn't seem like a very likely spot. What's this piece of land along the shoreline?"

"That's the estate, where we were the first night. Possible, I suppose, but both Audrey and Megan said Jimmy left, and there are neighbors nearby. I don't see how anything could have happened there."

"What about this big area over here?"

"That's hill country, southwest of the town," I said. "It's undeveloped, no houses. Loggers occasionally do some cutting up there, trees for the chipping plant, but that's about it."

"That sounds a little more like it. Is it fenced?"

"I'm not sure. I haven't been up there in years. As I recall, there are old logging trails in and out of it."

"Can I get in there with a car?"

"Sure. It might be difficult; the roads are pretty rough, but it's navigable, I suppose. The thing is, I don't think you realize how big an area we're talking about. It would take an army to search it all."

"I won't have to search it all. It was raining, remember, and Jimmy weighed one eighty. If he's up there, he'll be near a road. Where can I rent a car?"

"At the airport," I said. "The Rent-A-Wreck outfit in town might be cheaper, but I don't think you'd want to blunder around in the hills with one of theirs."

"The airport'll do fine."

"There's one thing you'd better keep in mind. A lot of the trails up there are visible from the town. You'll almost certainly be noticed, so be careful. Oh, and you'd better buy yourself a blaze orange vest. It'd be shame if a guy who's trying so hard to get killed on purpose got shish-kebabbed by accident."

"I'll bear it in mind," he said, smiling. "I really appreciate all the help you've given. But I'd like to ask one last favor—a big one."

"You can ask."

"Would you have dinner with me tonight? Please? My treat. And maybe we could talk about . . . something else. Anything."

I hesitated. I'd been half-expecting this. And I'd already made my decision. I was going to keep my distance. I had to. My life was complicated enough without someone new in it. And yet . . . .

15

GALLOWAY

DINNER WAS an oddly pleasant experience in a number of ways. For one thing, Red temporarily abandoned our mainstream menu and did something exotic with scampi and wild rice, with an avocado salad that was out of this world. I've known Red for a year, and I consider her as close a friend as I've ever had, yet she remains a constant surprise to me. I think if I were a lesbian, I'd consider marrying her. Assuming, of course, that she'd ask me.

Calderon was equally surprising. He was a good listener, a rare thing in a man. In anyone, really. With the subject of his brother's disappearance off limits, I found myself opening up, telling him about growing up as a tomboy, first in Detroit, then here in a North Woods town, trying to do a man's work from the time I was fifteen. I even told him about the financial jam I was in, and that it might mean the end of all I'd worked for during the past year. I think I rambled on too long. He was looking at me oddly. Probably waiting for me to hit him up for a loan.

"What?" I said.

"Nothing. No, something. The look in your eyes when you talk about this place. You really love it, don't you?"

"Love it?" I said surprised. "No, it's just a business, a way to um—no, that's not true. Maybe it was true in the beginning, that the Nest was only a means to an end, a way to make some kind of a life with my son and be able to dive without having to depend on it for a living. But I guess it's more than that now. Look at this building; knotty pine walls, hand-fitted when the Kaiser was in knee pants, or whatever they wore back then. And the beachfront deck I added last summer . . . Yeah, maybe I do love it a little. But if I have to, I can walk away from it. I've done harder things."

"Walking away's not so hard," he said, a faint shadow darkening his eyes. "I've walked away from things most of my life. It's what sailors do best, you know?"

"Leaving a girl in every port?"

"Hardly. What was it Groucho Marx said? I'd never join a club that would have me as a member? Something like that."

"Whoa, did I miss something? How did we get from girls to Groucho?"

"Simple. What self-respecting sailor would want to date a girl who'd date a sailor?"

"Mmmmm. And where does that leave me?"

"It doesn't apply. I'm not a sailor anymore. And this isn't a date, exactly." His smile faded. I followed his glance across the room to the door. Lizard: That was my first impression. A tall, gaunt lizard of a man, nearly chinless, sandy hair trimmed to barely more than a fuzz. He was wearing civilian clothes—a blue suit, light blue shirt, brown shoes spit-shined to a mirror gloss. He might as well have been in uniform. He scanned the room, spotted us, and stalked directly over, ramrod-stiff.

"Calderon," he said, his voice a flat rasp, "we need to talk."

"I'm not so sure we do, Galloway," Ray said evenly. "For one thing, I understand you've already done some talking. To the local sheriff. That wasn't a very bright move, was it?"

"It could have been the easy way, but we can do it any way we have to. Can we talk? Outside?"

"Sure," Ray said abruptly. "Let's do that. Excuse me a moment, Mitch. This won't take long."

He followed Galloway to the French doors out to the deck. And I thought about it for a moment and then casually wandered back to the kitchen and stood near the exhaust vent. And listened. Poor manners? Definitely. But if I've learned one thing from the diving trade that applies to the rest of life, it's what you don't know *can* hurt you. It may even kill you if you're not careful. Ergo, curiosity may be tough on cats, but it's a survival trait for working women.

Unfortunately, I couldn't hear all that much. Galloway did most of the talking, and his rasp was masked by the lap of the waves in the background. The tone of the conversation was clear enough, though. Galloway was leaning hard on Ray about something, threatening him with prison. He mentioned Leavenworth more than once. And he repeated a name several times. West? Best? Something like that. And then Galloway suddenly quit speaking in midsentence. I stepped to the window. In the shadows, they seemed to be embracing. . . . No, Ray had Galloway backed up against the railing, fists clamped on his lapels, their faces only inches apart. Then he released him abruptly, turned away, and stalked down the steps to the beach.

Galloway stood there unsteadily for a moment, staring after him. Then he straightened his tie, brushed his lapels off, and walked stiffly off around the building toward the parking lot.

I gave him a minute, then I slipped out the kitchen door and followed Ray down the beach. He was standing on the pier, arms folded, staring off into the dark.

"Hi," I said when I was still ten yards away. "Is everything all right?"

"Nope," he said quietly, without turning. "Nothing's right at all. Sorry about abandoning you. I thought I'd better cool off a minute before I rejoined civilization."

"That bad?"

"That bad. You wanna hear about it?"

"Absolutely."

"You're very direct, aren't you?" he said, turning, with the ghost of a smile.

"It's a self-defense. I'm lousy at mind games. What did Galloway want?"

"Me. I've got unfinished business back in Norfolk."

"What kind of business?"

"It doesn't matter now. None of it."

"I'd say the man came an awfully long way for something that doesn't matter. Are you in some kind of trouble?"

"Not yet, but I probably will be. He's a cop with the navy's Criminal Investigation Division. He can make my life complicated if he chooses to."

"How? I thought you weren't in the navy anymore."

"Technically, I'm not. Look, it comes down to this. A few months after my mother died, Jimmy got into a major jam with the shore patrol. He was running with a rough bunch, and he got mixed up with people who were dealing serious drugs on the base at Norfolk. In fact, it was during questioning that he learned they were still looking for his father, for God's sake. In any case, I flew back from the PI to—"

"PI?"

"Sorry, the Philippines. I was stationed there, air rescue. Anyway, I flew back to try to help Jimmy. And I cut a deal. They reduced his time to a few months plus parole, and in return I took a phony dishonorable discharge on a trumped-up drug deal so I'd look dirty enough to infiltrate the crew Jimmy was mixed up with. And it was working out pretty well, too well maybe. Until Jimmy decided to try to turn his life around by coming up here to find his father."

"What do you mean, it was working too well?"

"To be honest, I was having a helluva good time. I liked playing the role, fast cars, fast life. But at the same time, I knew I wasn't really part of it. I was one of the good guys. I got so wrapped up in the game, I kinda lost track of why I'd gotten into it in the first place. I'd agreed to to do it because Jimmy needed me. The thing is, he still did, only I was so busy playing narc, I didn't have time for him. And so he came up here, looking for somebody who might really give a damn about him."

"He must have known you cared about him."

"If I'd cared a little more, maybe he wouldn't have come up here at all. Maybe he'd still be alive. But either way, Galloway's problems with some sleazebag dopers back in Norfolk just don't seem very important anymore."

"You don't really think you're responsible for what happened to Jimmy, do you?"

"Yes and no. Jimmy came up here because I . . . failed him. I wasn't there for him when he needed me. And I guess I'll have to learn to live with that somehow. If I can. But what happened to him after he got here, no, that's not my fault. And maybe I can do something about that. At least I have to try."

"How?"

"For openers, I have to find Jimmy, somehow. I'll never convince anyone that he didn't just take off unless I can come up with some evidence. But even if I never prove anything, I still need to find him. For me, and for him. And I'm going to. No matter what it costs or who gets hurt. I can't let him down again this last time. I just can't. And there it is. So," he said, taking a ragged breath. "You offered to help earlier. Are you sure you still want to?"

I hesitated. He was very close. Too close. I wanted to touch his cheek. Instead, I took a deep breath and moved away from him. He was still a stranger to me. All we really had in common was a mutual lone-wolf wariness. And chemistry. Serious chemistry. The kind that makes differences seem unimportant—at first. I think I felt it the first time I saw him at the river. I'd been waiting for it to fade ever since. And yet, here we were. "I said I'd do what I can," I replied, keeping my voice remarkably cool, I thought. "I meant it. I still do."

"Thank you. That means a lot. It really does. Look, I'm sorry about all this. I was hoping to have a quiet dinner, maybe forget our troubles. Instead, mine seem to be hunting me down."

"It wasn't your fault, and look on the bright side. It gives us an excuse to try again."

74

"I'd like that."

"Yeah," I said. "I would, too."

"Soon?"

"We'll see," I said.

16

BACK FROM THE DEAD

THAT NIGHT, at my cottage on the point, I slept fitfully, popping in and out of drowsiness like a moth in a neon maze. I was bone tired, but every time I dropped off, some annoying fragment of memory would prod me awake. Ellen Maybry hesitantly telling me my loan probably wouldn't go through and that the Nest might not pass another safety inspection. I almost felt sorry for her. She seemed nearly as bothered by the situation as I was. A pity. It might have been easier to handle if I'd been able to personalize the rejection somehow, to dislike Ellen or her boss or . . . hell, anyone. But it wasn't that simple. It was just bad luck. Like being trampled by a herd of stampeding ducks. Wasn't it?

And when I tired of chewing on that problem and forced it back into its file slot, I'd suddenly see Ray grabbing Galloway by the lapels, snarling into his face. The gentleman had a temper, no doubt about it. I'd seen that fire in my father's eyes more than once. Maybe that was it. I was secretly attracted to Ray because he reminded me of my father.

Yeah, right.

Maybe I could get myself booked onto one of the freak-of-the-week TV talk shows—"Women Who Love Men Who Resemble Their Fathers." The idea was so ludicrous, I almost laughed aloud. I could just see it, Oprah or Phil shoving a microphone in my face, asking me when I'd first realized I loved—Oops, where had that word come from? My imaginary television show? Or perhaps a little closer to home?

Somehow, in the middle of the muddle, I must have dropped off. I could have sworn I was still trying to work out the Freudian triangle of Ray, my father, and television talk-show hosts, when the room was suddenly bathed in the gray light of morning. I tried to blot it out with my pillow, but it was too late. I was awake. Damn. I didn't feel as if I'd slept at all. And the grim light was a perfect tone for my mood.

I rolled out of bed with a groan, stumbled to the shower, set the water temperature one degree below death by scalding, then stood under it for a good ten minutes.

It helped. By the time I'd brushed my hair into place and pulled on my morning ensemble of jeans and a sweatshirt, I felt almost human. I was toasting an English muffin, waiting for the coffee to perk, when I heard a car crunch into my gravel driveway. Ray?

I peered out the kitchen window. A police car eased to a halt beside my Jeep and Charlie Bauer unfolded himself from behind the wheel.

"Good morning, Mitch. Hope I didn't wake you."

"Nope. I've been up for days. Is this business or pleasure?"

"Both. I mean, I'm here on business, but seeing you's always a pleasure."

"Uh-huh. It couldn't be that you can smell the coffee perking, could it? It's almost ready, so if you're going to read me my rights, at least wait until I'm awake, okay?"

"I'm not here to arrest you, though I don't doubt you deserve it for something or other," Charlie said, following me into the kitchen and taking a seat at my comfortably distressed oak table. He was glancing around with an odd mixture of unease and . . . satisfaction, I thought. I've gotten to know him fairly well over the past year, and I like him, but he's never an easy man to read.

"So what's up?" I said lightly, pouring two mugs of steam-

77

ing cinnamon coffee and carrying them to the table.

"Your friend Calderon. Have you seen him?"

"This morning, you mean? What the hell kind of a question is that?"

"Hey, no offense intended, Mitch. It's just that something came up early this morning. When I checked his motel, the clerk said Ray caught a cab to the airport last night, came back in a rented car, then went out again later. And didn't come back."

"And you thought he might have spent the night here?"

"It occurred to me," Charlie said, sipping his coffee, slightly flustered. "You two seem to hit it off pretty well."

"I hit it off fairly well with a lot of people. That doesn't mean I take them home to play house."

"Mitch, I didn't mean it that way."

"No? Calderon was out all night, so you come looking for him here first thing in the morning? Well, go ahead, Charlie, check under my bed. Is anybody else missing? Judge Crater? Jimmy Hoffa? Maybe they're back there playing pinochle."

"Look, please don't make a big thing out of this. I feel like enough of a schmuck already."

"You should. I thought we knew each other better than that."

"We do."

"And yet, here you are, right?"

"But not because I really thought Calderon would be here."

"No? Then why?"

"I don't know," Charlie said, sighing. "I guess I was just afraid he might be. Look, I admit it, I'm a jerk, okay? I apologize. So how about cutting me some slack? Have some pity for the mentally handicapped, if nothing else."

"I'll think about it. Why are you looking for Ray, anyway?"

"Gosh, I'm not sure I can tell you," he said, toying with me. He was trying not to look smug, and failing. "It's technically official business."

"Fine. In that case, you can take your official business on the road, Bauer. And leave your coffee. I only make it for friends."

"Okay, okay. No harm in telling you, I suppose. We've um . . . we've turned up his brother's body."

His face went out of focus for a moment, and the room tilted slightly. I half-expected my cup to slide off the table. "Where?" I managed.

"In Canada, actually," he said, with as broad a smile as I've ever seen on the man. "He's alive and well and walking around in Toronto."

"You're kidding."

"I couldn't be more serious. It came in over the line this morning about five A.M. So, do you have any idea where Ray might be?"

"Yes," I said, grinning like a total idiot. "I think I just might have."

17

REVELATION

THE MCCLAIN Industrial Fuels plant is north of Huron Harbor, a mile or so inland from the lakeshore. It occupies roughly half of a sprawling industrial-park complex that once housed a hardboard plant, a sawmill, and a number of satellite outfits that manufactured everything from shipping crates to prefab furniture legs. The crunch in the construction business had gutted the lot of them when the lumber and hardboard markets crashed, and now only the fuels plant remains. The complex that once had transmuted logs of aspen and ash into the makings of homes and furniture now chews them into chips to feed industrial furnaces downstate. Power to the people. And to General Motors, and Ford, and Chrysler, of course.

We found Ray's car parked in a turnout a half mile or so up the road from the plant, but Ray was nowhere in sight. We were trying to decide where to look when he made the question moot by strolling casually down from the crest of a brushy hill a hundred yards beyond the turnout.

He was wearing camouflage fatigues and hiking boots and carried a binocular case slung over his shoulder. He'd apparently been out all night; he looked a bit frayed and needed a shave.

Men can do that, stay out all night, grow a stubble, and still manage to look fashionably scruffy. There's no damned justice.

"Good morning," Charlie said affably. "Kind of early for sight-seeing, isn't it?"

"That depends on what you're looking for," Ray said with a shrug. "What are you two looking for?"

"You," Charlie said. "A cable came into the station for me this morning. I thought you might want to see it." He fished an envelope out of his jacket and handed it to Ray. As Ray read, I saw his breath catch for a moment, then he turned away, giving us his back. Charlie glanced at me and smiled, but I was too intent on watching Ray to give him more than a nod. When Ray finished reading, he stared off into the hills for a moment, getting his breathing under control. But when he turned to face us, I realized the emotion he was trying to contain wasn't joy. It was rage.

"Have you seen this?" he asked, offering me the cable.

"No." I took the sheet from him. It was a Western Union cable, addressed to the sheriff's department, Huron Harbor, from the Mayfair Hotel, Toronto, Ontario. From James Calderon. The note briefly described the area where his rental car could be found and apologized for any trouble he might have caused. He'd panicked after the accident and fled, but he would make full restitution as soon as he could. He asked Charlie to inform the rental-car company and any relatives who inquired that he'd contact them soon. Thanks. That was it.

"When did you get it?" Ray asked.

"It came in at five this morning over our fax. Tim Nance was on duty and rolled me out. Why?"

"Why?" Ray said, not bothering to conceal the contempt in his voice. "Jesus, Bauer, you can't be stupid enough to fall for this."

"Fall for what?" Charlie said, reddening. "I admit I was so grateful to be able to give somebody good news for a change that I haven't really thought much further, but offhand I don't see

81

any problem with it. We thought all along he might have just taken off—okay, so he wound up in Toronto. Is that such bad news?"

"It wouldn't be if it was true, but it's not. Are you sure you didn't whip this little scam up yourself?"

"Look, Calderon, I've cut you some slack, but I've taken about all the crap from you I'm going to, damn it—"

"Hold it, both of you," I said stepping between them. "Ray, I don't know what the trouble is here, but I do know Charlie wouldn't mislead you about something like this. Look, maybe I'm missing something here, but I don't understand. What do you think's wrong with this?"

"Everything's wrong with it," he snapped. "Toronto? Jimmy's car is in the river. So how did he get to Canada? Backstroke?"

"I expect he hitched a ride," Charlie said. "This isn't New York, *or* Norfolk," he added pointedly. "The roads get lonely and folks are a bit more trusting up here. Hitchhikers can cover a fair amount of ground."

"But all the way to Canada? And what's he been using for money?"

A shadow of doubt clouded Charlie's eyes.

"Mrs. McClain said she gave him some money," I put in reluctantly.

"That's right," Ray said acidly. "A few hundred, wasn't it? And it's been ten days. Ever spend any time in Toronto? Things are a little steep up there. Look, I don't want to debate this thing. It's bogus, and that's it."

"You've raised some valid points," Charlie admitted, "but none of them are absolute. Why are you so certain? At the very least, I'd think you'd *want* it to be genuine."

"Christ, don't you think I do?" Ray said. "For a second there . . . Ah, hell, it doesn't matter. It's not genuine. I wish to God it was, but it's not."

"Same question. Why are you so sure?"

"Because it was addressed to the wrong person," I said slowly. "Why would he contact you, Charlie? Why not Ray?"

"I don't know. And anyway, how do we know he hasn't tried to contact you? You've been up here for the past few days. Do you have an answering machine, or anyone who'd take your messages back in Norfolk?"

"No," Ray admitted, "but I've got something almost as good. Jimmy and I have bankcards for a joint account. He could make cash withdrawals from an automatic teller machine almost anywhere. He hasn't. I checked."

"Maybe he hasn't run short of cash yet."

"And maybe you're a little too goddamn reluctant to take my word on this," Ray said. "If this was legitimate, don't you think I'd know it?"

"Hell, I don't know what I think about this anymore," Charlie said, throwing up his hands. "If it's a fake—and I'm not altogether convinced it is—why send it at all?"

"Why do you think?" Ray said. "To draw me off."

"Maybe not," I said. "What happens now, Charlie? If Jimmy's in Canada, do you have a crime to investigate?"

"You're assuming he's actually been investigating," Ray snapped. "Personally, I've got some doubts about that."

Charlie's retort was cut off by the roar of a vehicle pulling into the car park. A silver-and-black McClain Industrial Fuels patrol car complete with roof-rack emergency lights slammed to a halt beside us and a tall, rawboned scarecrow in a gray uniform topped with black epaulets and cap stepped out: Pake Hemmerli—one of Hannah McClain's shirttail relatives. A stolid Finn, he was handsome enough to be a poster boy for beer or bowling shirts, but only the faintest light of intelligence showed in his sky-blue eyes.

"Sheriff, anything I can help you with?"

"Do I look like I need help?" Charlie said angrily.

"Not to me, no," Pake said, unoffended. "Captain McClain seen your car out here and sent me on to ask, is all. So I'm askin'."

"*Captain* McClain? Gordon's calling himself captain now?"

"It's just a job title, Charlie," Pake said, shrugging. "It's not like anybody has to salute him, though I imagine that'll be next.

83

What the hell, his name's McClain, like the sign over the plant gate, you know? Is this the Mex everybody's talkin' about?" he asked, nodding at Ray.

"Pake, no offense, but who I talk to is really none of your business. So tell your boss everything's under control here and go back to whatever it is you guys do over there. Read me?"

"Whatever you say, Charlie. It's nothin' to me one way or the other," Pake said easily. He folded himself back into his cruiser and fired it up. But I noticed he took a long look at Ray, memorizing his features, before he dropped the patrol car into gear and rumbled off.

"Gordon McClain?" Ray asked. "Owen's brother?"

"That's right," Charlie acknowledged. "Owney made him head of plant security, probably as much to keep him out of trouble as anything else."

"You've known him a long time, then?"

"That's right, Mr. Calderon, a long time. I've even arrested him. More than once, in fact. Is that what you were doing out here, hoping to get a look at Gordon?"

"Right now, I'm more interested in what you're going to do about this cable," Ray said, tossing it to him.

"I'm not sure I should do anything. You think it's fake, fine, that's your opinion, but I have no reason to believe it is. And as Mitch pointed out, we don't have a crime here. All I've been investigating is a missing persons case. If there's a possibility your brother's alive, then my next move would be to ask the Toronto police to keep an eye out for him as a courtesy. At the moment, he's only wanted for leaving the scene of an accident, and we can't even extradite for that."

"How about falsifying evidence in a murder investigation?" Ray said. "Does that qualify as a crime?"

"It might," Charlie conceded. "But I'm not certain that's actually the case."

"Charlie, this is a Western Union cable, right?" I said. "And you said it came in over your fax machine?"

"That's right. Telegrams aren't really cables anymore—they fax 'em, phone 'em, whatever's most convenient."

"But this one was sent from a hotel. The Mayfair? Couldn't you fax them back? Send Jimmy's picture over the line. If someone recognizes it, we know he's there. If not, well, at least you know more than you do now."

Charlie eyed me neutrally for a moment, then nodded. "It might not prove anything, but I guess it's worth a try. On one condition."

"Which is?"

"I want you to come to the station, Calderon, and watch me send it. I don't want any questions about it afterward, if you follow me. And if the Western Union people confirm the ID, I expect you'll want to catch the next flight north. Correct?"

"Yeah," Ray agreed. "I probably will. If they confirm the ID."

"Good. So why don't we find out."

18
STATION BREAK

THE HURON Harbor sheriff's department is in the older section of town, near the harbor, housed in the basement of the county courthouse. The courthouse itself is a wonderful turn-of-the-century poured-concrete edifice with fluted columns, oaken doors, and a bronze dedication plate the size of a Volkswagen beside the entrance. The sheriff's department is another matter: strictly utilitarian, concrete walls and floors either bare or painted battleship gray. The gunmetal gray desks and counters look like army surplus—World War I, say, or maybe the Franco-Prussian.

Tim Nance was on duty at the counter, a jug-eared mule of a man nearly as tall as Charlie. His brush cut was steel gray and matched the metal frames of his glasses. The few times I'd met him, I'd gotten the impression his head was equally hard. He glowered at Ray and me as we followed Charlie back to his office, though it probably wasn't anything personal. I'd never seen him with any other expression.

"Charlie," he called after us, "you've got a message here from the high school principal. They had a break-in last night."

"I'll talk to him later. Better yet, why don't you drive over there, check it out. I'll hold the fort."

"My shift's over in half an hour," Nance protested.

"Then you'd best get a move on, *Officer* Nance. I've got problems of my own." Charlie closed the door on Nance's grumbling. His office was as Spartan as the rest of the station, a pair of bile green filing cabinets against one wall and a battered metal desk with a typewriter on it—not a computer, just an honest-to-God Underwood. It wasn't even electric, and somehow it suited Charlie to a tee.

"Okay, here's the drill," he said, turning to face us. "I'll ring Western Union in Toronto, try to connect with whoever took the message at their end. I'll do the whole thing on my speakerphone, up front and personal, so there's no question about what's happening. Any questions?"

"Suppose the operator or whatever is off duty?" Ray asked.

"Then we'll try again later, same rules. Okay?"

Ray shrugged. Charlie checked the cable, then tapped out the number on his phone.

"Western Union." The voice over the speakerphone was female, cheerful, and metallicized, like a play-by-play announcer at a distant stadium.

"This is Sheriff Charles Bauer, Huron County, Michigan. My office received a fax from your folks at five A.M. Is the operator who sent it still on duty?"

"I surely am," she replied. "Will be until noon. Is there a problem?"

"That depends. Could I please have your name, miss?"

"It's Mrs., actually. Clare Leblanc. If you wish to talk to the manager, he comes on at noon."

"I don't think that'll be necessary," Charlie said. "I only need a little information, Mrs. Leblanc. Do you remember the man who cabled my office this morning?"

"I remember the person, yes. We don't do a lot of business at five A.M. She was my only customer until an hour or so ago."

"She?"

"Right you are. It was a woman, Sheriff."

"You're certain?"

"I have three children, Sheriff Bauer. I know the difference between boys and girls."

"Sorry. Did you know her?"

"Never saw her before," Mrs. Leblanc said briskly, "but I can tell you she isn't a guest of the hotel. She paid cash; guests charge their messages to their rooms."

"Cash? Not a credit card?"

"I'm afraid not."

"Can you describe her?" Charlie asked.

"Um, I'm no expert, but I suppose so. She was young, mid-twenties or so, quite pretty in a scruffy sort of way."

"What do you mean by 'scruffy'?"

"You know, jeans with the knees torn out, a leather jacket, and a beret. Sunglasses. She was brunette, I think."

"Sunglasses? At five A.M.?"

"Nothing odd about that. Kids wear 'em round the clock nowadays, eh?" Was there anything else? I do have customers waiting."

"Just one last thing. Was she a Canadian or an American?"

"Sheriff, I'm surprised at you. We're *all* North Americans," the voice chided with a hint of mischief. "Some of you are just . . . lower than the rest of us, eh? But to answer your question, she was a Yank. She paid in Canadian currency, and from her accent, I'd guess she's lived here awhile, but she was definitely a Yank. And I really do have to go. If you need anything further, call me anytime between four A.M. and noon, and I'll be happy to talk your ear off."

"Thank you, Mrs. Leblanc. You've been a big help."

"You're welcome. Come up and see us sometime." The phone clicked off as she broke the connection.

"Damn," Charlie said softly.

"Surprised?" Ray said. "I'm not."

"I'm not surprised, exactly. I was just hoping for something conclusive."

"How conclusive does it have to be? I told you Jimmy didn't send that cable, and he didn't."

"And the girl? It hadn't occurred to you that since he was, in effect, confessing to a crime, he might have had someone send it for him?"

"Like his girlfriend, you mean? He doesn't know anybody up there."

"You can't be sure about that, Mr. Calderon. You know how young people are. He could've made a dozen friends in a week."

"Not a chance," Ray said. "Jimmy won't be making any more friends. Look, don't worry about it, Charlie. You wanted an excuse to drop the search and you've got it. Just don't expect me to buy into your little song and dance."

"You really are a prize, you know that, Calderon? I've already taken more crap off you than—"

"Hold it," I interrupted. "I'm not dressed for this."

"For what?" Charlie snapped.

"For being a referee," I said, exasperated. "Don't I need a zebra-striped shirt or something? Look, I don't know if we've learned anything this morning or not, but I know a little breather to think it over won't hurt anything. And anyway, I'm a working woman and I need to get going. Ray, can you give me a lift?"

"Why not? I'm not getting a damned thing accomplished here."

"Thank you, kind sir. Your graciousness underwhelms me. I'll talk to you later, Charlie. And thanks for the front-row seat, even if the show turned out to be a bomb."

19

THE LONGEST MILE

"WHERE ARE you going?" Ray called after me as I stalked away from the courthouse. "My car's in the lot."

"I've changed my mind; I'd rather walk. I need to cool off."

"Well, so do I. Mind if I join you?" he said, falling into step beside me.

"I'm not sure. You're the reason I need to cool off."

"Me? What did I do?"

"The same thing you've been doing since you got here," I said, turning to face him. "Take a look around you. What do you see?"

"A town," he said, glancing around. "What's your point?"

"That *is* my point," I said. "It's a town, a little lakeshore town in the north country, twelve thousand souls, not counting tourists. It may only be a flyspeck on a map of the world, but it's *my* town. I grew up here and I'm living here now because I choose to. And I know you've had a rough time since you came here, but you're not helping things by automatically assuming that anyone who doesn't see things your way must be part of a damned conspiracy."

"I don't think that; it's just . . . Ah, hell, maybe it does seem that way sometimes. You're talking about Sheriff Bauer, aren't you?"

"About Charlie and nearly everyone else," I said, resuming my stride, not much caring whether Ray followed or not. We were in the old business district now. It had once been the center of town, but new JC Penney's and Wal-Mart malls south of the city had absorbed most of the stores that needed pedestrian traffic to survive. The only shops left now were artsy-craftsy boutiques, bookstores, a candelaria, a holistic drugstore, a couple of art galleries. Yuppie heaven.

"Okay, okay," Ray said, catching up. "Look, maybe you're right. Maybe I was out of line. If you want me to apologize to Bauer, I will."

"If you want to apologize for being a jerk back there, be my guest. But don't do me any favors."

"Look, I said I was sorry, and I am. I'd get down on my knees, but you're walking too damned fast."

"For that, I'll stop," I said, turning to face him. "Well?"

"You don't really want me to get down on my knees, do you?"

I thought about it. "No," I said, walking away at a more reasonable pace. "But I admit, the idea has some appeal."

"Will you settle for me buying Charlie a drink sometime and making nice."

"Do you know how to make nice?"

"Yeah," he said, taking a deep breath. "I'm a little rusty at it, but I do know how. Lately I haven't had much reason to try. Not to make excuses, but this thing's got me half-crazy."

"Why do I have the feeling you were at least half-crazy before?"

"Because you're an intelligent, perceptive woman," he said, smiling. The first smile I'd seen all morning. A bit strained, perhaps, but a nice smile all the same. "I probably was half-crazy, which makes it all the worse. I just can't seem to get a handle on anything, Mitch. I feel like I'm blundering around blindfolded in a bat cave."

"Well try to avoid blundering into Charlie, okay? He's not your enemy. He's doing his best. And if you and I are going to be friends, I don't want to keep getting caught in the cross fire between you two."

"Fair enough, no more cross fire. Next time, we'll step into the alley and settle it like men."

"What?"

"I'm kidding, Mitch. Jeez, I was only kidding, honest. I may be a brick or two shy of a load, but I'm not that crazy."

"Maybe you're just tired. How long were you out there last night?"

"Most of the night. I got there about ten."

"And? What did you see?"

"Trucks, trucks, and then a little later I saw some trucks. Flatbeds loaded with logs coming in and semitrailers with what I assume were loads of whatever they make there going out. I couldn't be sure; the trailers were covered with tarps."

"State law—all open trailers have to be covered."

"In any case, there was a lot of activity all night: trucks loading and unloading, people moving around, plus security guards on patrol. I don't think anything could happen out there without attracting a crowd; it's just too busy. It was a long shot anyway. Maybe I'll have better luck in the hills."

"I see. You won't even consider the possibility that Charlie's telegram might be legitimate?"

"I've already considered it. For a moment out there by the plant when he handed me the cable, I was . . . overwhelmed. My heart was pounding and . . . then reality, or whatever, set in, and I knew it was a con. Jimmy wouldn't have cabled Bauer about that car. He'd never done anything that responsible in his life. If he'd actually cracked it up and managed to get out somehow, he would have dusted himself off, reported it stolen, and then gone on about his business. Then, even if someone found it later, he'd be covered. No problems with the police or his parole officer. Home free."

"Not a very flattering theory," I said.

"Look, I loved my brother, but I didn't have many illusions about him. He was a screwup with a major talent for trouble," but . . . he wasn't a bad guy. I think he would have gotten himself squared away eventually. We'll never know now. I'll never know. Someone stole his last chance. Maybe his birth father. But definitely someone with serious cash on hand."

"Why do you say that?"

"The fax was from Toronto—and on short notice. That kind of service doesn't come cheaply. They were hoping I'd go charging off on a wild-goose chase. It'll be interesting to see what happens when I don't."

"It might also be dangerous."

"It might. Especially for my friends."

"What friends are those?"

"You, Mitch. You're it, the only friend I've got. Unless you've decided to dump me for being a jerk."

"The thought had crossed my mind."

"Really?" He stopped and so did I, facing each other on the sidewalk. "In that case . . ." he said. And he kissed me. On the mouth. On Park Street. In front of the drugstore. An older couple walked around us, smiling. And the earth didn't move, exactly, and I didn't see fireworks. But I might have if our kiss had lasted one second longer. I stepped back.

"What do you think you're doing?" I said.

"Saying good-bye, probably. I've wanted to do that for a while now, and I was afraid I might not get another chance. So I'm sorry if I . . . upset you, but not for the kiss. If you want to pop me one for it, go ahead. Are you angry?"

"I don't know," I lied. "Look, I'm late for work," I said, turning away to mask my confusion. "I'll see you around."

"How about tonight? At the Nest?"

"We're open to the public," I said. At the time, it was true.

20

THE INSPECTOR

THE NEST was moderately busy when I wandered in about eleven. There were a dozen or so shift workers at the bar, unwinding with a brew and conversation after their long night on the job, and a few tables of shop girls and office workers grabbing an early lunch. One of the long tables in the main dining room was filled with a half a dozen men in suits, having a lunch conference, or maybe a celebration, judging from the volume and ribald good cheer.

Red was less cheery. I found her in the kitchen with Irma, the cook, assembling ham and cheese croissandwiches with harried efficiency.

"I'll take over here," I offered. "Go make nice with the tipping customers."

"You don't have time. Didn't you see him?"

"Who?"

"The gentleman who was waiting outside for you when I opened this morning. His name's Winarski. Emil, I think he said."

"I don't know him."

"You will. He's in the main dining room. Fiftyish, cheap blue suit. He'll be the guy on top of the stepladder. With the clipboard."

94

"Sweet Jesus," I said softly.

"Not even close," Red said. "Jesus wouldn't need a ladder."

He was in the far corner of the dining room, away from the other customers, thank God. He was just climbing down the ladder when I found him, a small man, stoop-shouldered, with a weathered face streaked with broken veins. His suit was a few sizes too large, as though he'd inherited it from his grandfather. Or perhaps it had fit him once, before life had worn him down. He didn't notice me, or pretended not to. He jotted a few notes on his clipboard, then began sliding the ladder along to the next beam.

"Hi," I said. "I'm Michelle Mitchell. Red said you were looking for me."

"Yes, ma'am," he said shyly, offering his gnarled hand. "I'm Emil Winarski. I'm the county building inspector, or one of 'em anyways. You're the owner?"

"That's right."

"Thought you must be," he said, nodding. "I knew your dad, years ago. You favor him some. Prettier, though," he added hastily. "I meant, well, you're tall, like him. For a girl, I mean. He was um . . . he was quite a character, Shan was. We weren't buddies or nothing, didn't hang around together, but . . . I knew him. Bought fishin' tackle and such from him. Quite a character. He left you this place, huh?"

"That's right."

"Well, I'm sorry to say it, but it looks to me like he left you more'n a few problems along with it."

"You mean the roof? It leaks a little, but it's not serious. I've already made plans to have it fixed when things slow down a little after hunting season."

"I, um . . . I'm afraid it's not quite that simple, Ms. Mitchell."

"Call me Mitch; everybody does. And why isn't it that simple, Mr. Winarski?"

"Some of those beams up there," he said, avoiding my eyes. "They got the dry rot."

"I'm aware of that. I plan to replace them when I have the roof repaired. So what's the problem?"

"The problem is, I can't let you wait that long, ma'am. I'm going to have to close you down right away. Some of those beams look . . . unsafe to me."

"Unsafe?" I echoed, not bothering to conceal my disbelief. "You've got to be kidding. They're nearly ten inches thick. Even if they were rotted half through—and they aren't—there's still more solid support left up there than most modern buildings have to begin with."

"I know it may seem like it to a . . . person like yourself, ma'am—"

"Don't patronize me, Winarski. I know which end of a hammer to hold. I've repaired boats and I've remodeled houses, and I know enough about construction to know that if you drove a truck headfirst into this building, it'd bounce off. And you know it, too. If I thought for a second this building was unsafe, I'd close it in a New York minute. It's not. So what's really the problem here?"

"I'm sorry, ma'am," he said, and I believe he meant it. "But it's like I said. I'm going to have to close you down."

I bit off the tirade that was bubbling just below the surface. "When?" I said.

"Immed—no, wait. I can give you a week," he said hopefully. "Maybe you can . . . work something out."

"Work something out? I can't possibly have the repairs done in a week."

"No, ma'am, I know. But at least it might be enough time to make some kind of arrangements."

I stared at him, beginning to understand. "Arrangements?" I echoed. "Not repairs? What's that supposed to mean, exactly?"

"Ma'am, I don't know, I'm just . . . doing my job. Look, I've gotta go. I'm sorry."

"Stop by again anytime," I said. "It's always good to see my dad's old *friends.*"

He stopped, stung. "Lady," he said, turning to face me. "I

said I was sorry, and I am. But you've gotta understand, it ain't just me. I've got two boys. They're like me, you know, not much schooling, do mostly manual labor, but they're gettin' by all right now. They've got good jobs."

"I'm happy for them," I said. "What's that got to do with my problem?"

He shook his head. "I can give the week, Ms. Mitchell, but that's truly the best I can do."

"Is it? Mr. Winarski, why did you suddenly decide to inspect the Nest? I've been here a year. Why did you just happen to come today?"

"We um . . . we usually inspect the buildings every other year. By area, you know? All the buildings in one block, or on the same street."

"And are you inspecting other buildings on this street?"

"No, ma'am, I'm not. Sometimes, when we . . . have complaints, we have to look into 'em."

"You're saying someone complained?"

He nodded. "Something like that."

"Who?"

"I'm sorry, but that's confidential, ma'am. Really it is."

"I see."

"Yeah, I expect you do. Old Shan, he was pretty quick on the uptake, too. You know, when I was younger, I used to work in the woods, lumberin'. Swung a chain saw eight, ten hours a day. Got paid piecework. Didn't make much, but it wasn't a bad life. I liked being' out in the wind, the smell of the pines. I didn't wear a suit to work then. I liked that better, too."

He turned and walked away. I wanted to be angry at him, but I couldn't manage it. The life he was living and the way he felt about it was punishment enough.

"What's the verdict?" Red asked, coming up behind me.

"Guilty," I said. "We have a week to put our affairs in order, and then they close us down. Probably permanently, since I haven't a snowball's chance of raising the money. Tell me, when Winarski came in, where did he start his inspection?"

97

"Right where you found him. He came into the kitchen, asked to borrow a ladder, and went straight to the dining room. He seemed to know what he was looking for."

"He did. He said someone had filed a complaint."

"A complaint? About the roof? But how could they know? I swear to God, Mitch, I haven't talked to anybody about this."

"Maybe not, but I have," I said grimly. "And I think it's time we had another little chat."

21

BREAKING THE BANK

IT WAS a six-block walk to the bank. Which was just as well. I'd stormed out of the Nest, my head filled with visions of Ellen Maybry tied to a stake, with crumpled loan applications piled up to her nose, while I capered gaily about flicking my dad's battered Zippo. Okay, so it was a tad melodramatic. Maybe I'd just stand in the crowded bank lobby pointing my finger at her and yell a lot about trust and . . . what, exactly?

Halfway to the bank, my pace slowed a bit and my temper cooled enough to allow rational doubt to creep in. Ellen was the only person I could think of who could have set me up for the building inspector, but what possible reason would my friendly neighborhood loan officer have for selling me out? Aside from a few competitors up and down the shore, I couldn't think of a soul who'd gain anything by getting the Nest closed down. And yet Winarski had all but admitted he was getting his arm twisted to lean on me.

But by whom? I had my suspicions, but that's all they were. Maybe Calderon's paranoia was contagious. But then again, maybe not. Being paranoid doesn't necessarily mean that people *aren't* out to get you, and someone had gone to considerable lengths to cause me trouble. Still, I wasn't likely to learn much by marching into the bank and blowing my stack. Besides, there was at least the ghost of a chance that I was mistaken.

I slowed my pace even more, trying to think of a ruse for getting Ellen alone for a serious chat. The alley behind the bank would have been my preference, but I was stumped for an approach. And then lady luck intervened.

As I approached the bank, my favorite loan person came waddling out of the front door with her purse over her shoulder and her bun in the oven. And I had to admit it, she not only looked gloriously pregnant, she looked innocent, too. So I put thoughts of throttling her aside, temporarily, and simply fell into step beside her.

"Hi, breaking for lunch?"

"Oh, hi, Miss Mitchell," she said with a quick smile. "No, I eat at my desk these days; restaurants are too great a temptation. I'm already as big as a house, and if I'm not careful, I'll end up barn-sized."

"I remember the feeling," I said. "It eases later."

"How much later?"

"A decade or so. Maybe two."

"That's a great comfort to hear," she said dryly. "I'm afraid my news isn't quite as encouraging. About your loan, I mean."

"No? What about it?"

"The board tabled it. I . . . was afraid they might."

"Well, you warned me my chances weren't very good. And the point may be academic anyway now. I had a visitor this morning—Emil Winarski."

"The building inspector?"

"You do know him, then?"

"I know who he is. I see his name on paperwork almost every day. But . . . you mean he did an inspection on the Nest?"

"That's right, and we flunked. You seem surprised."

"I am, a little. Technically, inspectors can show up anytime, but you took over the business only last year, and they must have done an inspection before the title and licenses could change hands. Why would they inspect you again so soon?"

"I don't know. I thought you might."

"Me? Why?"

"In a nutshell, Mrs. Mabry, my problems at the Nest haven't exactly been public knowledge. In fact, aside from my manager and myself, no one knew about the situation but you. I applied for a loan, and this morning I had a surprise visit from Mr. Winarski. You see where I'm going with this, don't you?"

"That's just not possible," she said firmly. "We're very cautious about protecting any information we acquire. No one at the bank has access to loan applications but the officers who deal with them. In your case, I was the only one who saw that paperwork."

"Which you passed on to the loan board?"

"Yes, but, Miss Mitchell, they're all citizens with impeccable credentials. Frankly, most of them are wealthy enough so that the temptation to use any insider information wouldn't even come up."

"Who are they?"

She hesitated. "Technically, that's confidential information. They're entitled to privacy."

"I thought I was, too, but someone certainly violated mine. You said once you wanted to see women do well in business. Well, I'm a businesswoman, and I need some help. If someone on your board used my application to do me in, I'm entitled to know about it."

"I can't give you the names of the board members. I'm sorry. But . . ."

"But?"

She took a deep breath. "One board member did seem to take more than a . . . casual interest in your application. I can't give you his name, but um . . . he's the newest member of the board. He . . . he took over his mother's seat when she retired."

"His mother's . . . You mean Owen McClain, Jr., don't you?" I said slowly.

"I really can't confirm that," she said, nodding an affirmation. "You understand, I'm sure."

"Oh yes," I said. "I think I'm beginning to."

22

The Jaws of Death

I'D BEEN inside Huron Harbor's industrial park only once, when I was a high school sophomore—on career day. Not that I expected to work there, nor did any of the girls on the excursion. The only jobs open to women at the hardboard plant or the industrial-pallet factory were secretarial, and you don't need to tour a plant to know what a typewriter looks like. Still, it was in the spring of the year, some of my friends' fathers worked at the place, and in those days I would have happily donated blood to skip a school day.

How many years ago? Thirteen? Fourteen? I couldn't quite make it compute. But though my memory of that last visit was a little hazy, I could see a lot had changed.

I'd borrowed Red's pickup truck for the drive over. The park was completely fenced now, a giant prison yard carved out of a series of low hills along the lakeshore. The fence was only six feet high, sufficient to keep animals and kids out, but anyone who was serious about getting onto the grounds could probably do it, though I couldn't imagine why they'd want to.

The back of the yard opened onto the lakeshore. There were old loading docks built along a narrow inlet where the chilly waters hammered the beach, but they obviously hadn't been used in years. Lake freighters used to load lumber and hardboard there for delivery to other Great Lakes ports like Chicago or Erie. Some even made the run out the Saint Lawrence Seaway to Europe or Mexico or South America. I used to dream about those freighters, dark shapes ghosting along in the moonlight. I didn't dream of working aboard them or even being a passenger, only of the ships themselves, going hull-down over the horizon, bound for . . . anywhere.

But they were only memories now, those ships, shadows in a young girl's dream. The monster trucks Ray had mentioned were the new reality, huge semis hauling flatbed trailers loaded with logs going in, passing other trucks coming out loaded with . . . whatever this place actually made.

Fortunately, the entrance road divided early on. The trucks were shunted down a side road to unload on the south end of the yard, while I followed a more circuitous route around to the entrance gate. It looked like a border crossing into Bulgaria. A large concrete blockhouse, newly built, had replaced the single phone booth–sized guardhouse I remembered. It had a McClain Industries sign nearly thirty feet high mounted on the roof. A yellow-and-black-striped crash bar the size of a telephone pole blocked the entrance gate. It looked heavy enough to keep out a tank or a Volkswagen loaded with hippie protesters, or whatever it was they were afraid of here. I eased Red's pickup to a halt beside the blockhouse, and Pake Hemmerli came trotting out, looking like an Aryan recruiting poster in his neatly tailored silver-and-black uniform. I rolled down the window.

"Pass, please, ma'am."

"I don't have a pass. I'm Michelle Mitchell, here to see Owney McClain."

"Do you have an appointment?"

"Nope, but if you tell him I'm here, I think he'll see me."

"I don't know," Pake said doubtfully. "Mr. McClain's pretty busy."

"And so are you, and so am I, and so are the guys in the cars who are starting to pile up behind me. So why don't you check

103

with Owney, and I'll be out of your hair one way or the other."

"Okay," he said, straightening. "Pull off to the side, please. This may take some time."

"No," I said.

"What?"

"I'll just stay where I am, thanks. Things may move along a little faster that way."

"You can't do that."

"I'm already doing it. And unless you think you can get a tow truck out here from town faster than you can get your boss on the phone, why don't you just make the call, okay?"

Pake opened his mouth to protest, then closed it without speaking and trotted back inside the building. I glanced in my rearview mirror. Two cars were in line behind me now and I could see a third on the way. Good.

Pake came back out of the building with another guard, a heavier-set type with silver braid on his cap and stars on his epaulets. Gordon McClain, Owney's uncle. I could have picked him out as a McClain even I hadn't seen Megan's sketch of him a few nights earlier. There was a strong family resemblance. He looked like Owney, add twenty years and a hundred-plus pounds.

"What's the problem here?"

"I imagine Pake already explained the situation. I'm waiting to see Owney."

"What's your business with Mr. McClain?"

"That's exactly what it is," I said, exasperated. "It's my business. For crying out loud, what's the holdup? I could get my appendix out faster than this."

"We might be able to arrange that, too," Gordon said, giving me his best take on a glower. It looked like indigestion. Someone behind me in line tapped his horn. It seemed to make up Gordon's mind.

"I'll escort you in," he said. "But if Owney doesn't want to see you, that's it. And we have our own tow trucks right here."

"I'm surprised you don't have antiaircraft guns, too," I said as he slid in beside me. "Why all the security?"

"Technology," he said brusquely. "This is a state-of-the-art plant. Industrial espionage is a major problem nowadays."

"So I've heard," I said, gunning Red's truck under the rising barrier. "I just wasn't aware that whacking up trees for firewood was exactly high-tech. Didn't the Chippewas heat their wicki-ups pretty much the same way?"

He let it pass. I felt his eyes on me, crawling around like sand fleas. "Go ahead and say it," I said. "I look like my dad. Everybody says so. You two were about the same age, weren't you?"

"Park in front of the main office," he growled. "Use one of the handicapped spots. You won't be here long and it'll save us a walk."

I parked at the end of the row, pointedly bypassing up the slots with wheelchair logos. The building was long and low, a single-story cinder-block bunker with a brick facade, World War II vintage.

A matronly grandmom type in an orchid print dress was seated at an information desk in the lobby. Gordon brusquely waved off her cheerful hello with what he thought was a show of authority. It didn't work. Rudeness never impresses me much. I glanced back to give her a raised eyebrow of apology, and she rolled her eyes. A universal woman's sign for "Men, hmph."

I followed Gordon down a broad carpeted hallway. Halfway along it, he stopped at an ornately carved double door, rapped once, and opened it for me.

It was a magnificent office, floor-to-ceiling bookcases, a massive Victorian desk, high-backed leather chairs deep enough to nap in. Owney McClain was on the phone, negotiating some kind of a deal, batting around figures of a hundred grand here, two hundred there. His coat was draped over his chair back. He was wearing a black pinstriped vest, his shirtsleeves were rolled up, and his tie was loosened. Just a casual North Woods country boy working a million-dollar deal.

Yet somehow it didn't seem quite real. I eased down in one

of the chairs facing his desk, trying to put my finger on what was triggering my phony-alarm, the warning buzzer that goes off whenever some clown I've just met starts talking about my eyes.

Two things struck me as odd. The room, for openers. Owney was a high school jock once. He was past it now. He was out of shape and his hair was thinning; still, every guy I've met who *ever* played sports will find a way to work it into the conversation in the first sixty seconds. Maybe it's genetic. In any case, this office had no trophies on display, no photographs. Ergo, either this wasn't really Owney's office, or at least the decor wasn't his choice. His mother's? Possibly. It was the kind of room a businesswoman would choose. All business. Abandon your humanity at the door.

And after a moment of listening to his end of the conversation, I realized that Owney himself didn't ring true. The vest was a good fit, his Rolex probably cost more than my Jeep, and yet there was uncertainty in his eyes and his tone, like a salesman down to his last deal. I noticed he'd missed a spot shaving, and there was a reddened area just above his ear he was scratching unconciously as he spoke. By the time he hung up, I wasn't at all certain there'd been anyone on the other end.

He rested his elbows on the desk, bridged his fingertips, and gazed over them at me. He was waiting for me to say something. I let him wait. "So," he said at last, "Uncle Gordon said you wanted to see me. What about?"

"I had a visit from the county building inspector this morning. He's going to close my business in a week."

"That's unfortunate."

"I think so, too. I also think you sent him around after you'd seen my loan application. Why would you do that?"

"Maybe we don't like the company you've been keeping," Gordon said.

"That occurred to me," I said, "but it seems a bit extreme, don't you think?"

"There's an old Ojibwa proverb," Gordon said. "When bears fight, the grass is trampled."

"That's very profound," I said. "Let me get this straight—you guys think you're bears, and I'm grass, is that it? Terrific. Look, I won't try to blow smoke about this. Having the Nest closed could cause me serious financial problems, as you're no doubt aware. What's the bottom line here? What is it you think you want?"

"Nothing complicated," Owney said. "Your new friend is sneaking around asking questions about my family and upsetting people. He was even spotted outside the plant early this morning, spying on it with binoculars. I don't know what he thinks he's doing, but I'm tired of being harassed. Plus, I understand he received word his brother isn't even around here anymore, that he's definitely out of the country."

"How could you know that? Or did you arrange it?"

"Don't be ridiculous. I heard about it, that's all. I have friends all over this county."

"Like the building inspector?"

"I don't recall ever meeting the gentleman, but I believe one of his sons works here. Is that right, Gordon?"

Gordon nodded. "Two of 'em, actually. Pulp cutters."

"You see, there you are. Even though I don't know Mr. Winarski personally, it's possible I could put in a good word for you, Mitch. If I had any reason to."

"Such as?"

"I want Calderon gone, Mitch. I want him away from my family, out of this county, preferably out of this state. And I want you either to convince him to go or to arrange things so that he can . . . be convinced."

"Arrange things? Meet him at the movies wearing a red dress, you mean? Something like that?"

"This is no laughing matter, Mitch."

"Believe me, Owney, I don't see anything funny about it, either. But I don't see how I can help you. I don't have that kind of influence with Calderon. I doubt that anyone has."

"Suppose we could arrange a . . . financial settlement, for yourself, I mean. One that you could . . . pass along to a friend, if you choose. My attorneys tell me I'd be ill-advised to deal with Calderon directly, something about an assumption of liability. They tell me I should just stay away from him. I'll be honest, that's not my style. Personally, I'd just as soon . . . Well, it doesn't matter. The point is, I can't talk to him about this, but you can."

"How much of a settlement are we talking about?" I asked.

"I was thinking of a round figure, say ten thousand? And another five for yourself. *If* Calderon takes the offer."

"I'll deliver the offer," I said, rising. "I can't guarantee his answer."

"It had better be yes," Gordon said, "or you're going to find yourself looking for work."

"You're right. Fortunately, I know of an opening: research assistant to Ray Calderon. He can use the help, and I'll have nothing better to do with my time."

"That would be a mistake."

"You've got to be kidding. I'll already have lost everything I own. The only thing I'll have left will be getting even. And I'll make it my full-time job."

"Mitch, now wait a minute," Owney said, blinking anxiously. "We've known each other a long time—"

"No, we haven't," I said, cutting him off. "We've been acquainted for a long time. I didn't have any idea of who you really were until today. I'll get back to you on this if we have anything further to talk about. Otherwise, count me out."

"That's exactly what we'll do," Gordon said. "Let her go, Owney. She's not worth the trouble. Come on, lady, I'll see you out."

I followed him out of the office door, so angry that I didn't realize until we were halfway along the hall that Gordon had turned the wrong way as we'd left the office.

I stopped. "This isn't the way we came in."

"I know. There's something I'd like you to see while you're here. It'll only take a minute. Nothing to worry about."

"Right," I said, following him. Worry? I half-hoped he would get out of line. I was dying to kick *something*. Still, there was something ominous about the hallway. And I realized it was a sound, a low, barely audible rumble, like a warning growl from deep in the belly of a beast.

The hall ended at two sets of heavy metal doors. They seemed more appropriate for a prison than a factory, but I realized why they were necessary as soon as Gordon opened them. The rumble in the hallway immediately doubled in volume. And then we stepped out onto a platform that overlooked the plant floor.

The noise was horrendous, a constant bestial thunder, like a herd of bulldozers having an orgy. It was absolutely unnerving, as was the sheer size of the place. The factory floor was the length of a football field and twice as wide. A monstrous train-sized machine, bright red and surprisingly clean, stretched the length of the building. It even looked a bit like a train, one taking on massive wooden passengers.

At the south end of the floor, trucks backed onto a platform and a hard hat at the controls of a set of pincers pushed the logs onto a mammoth conveyor belt. The belt carried them through a watery mist into the mouth of the machine. What happened to them in its bowels, I couldn't even imagine. Midway along, I could see flames flickering from somewhere within its belly, and at the far end of it a second conveyor belt poured out a torrent of charred wood chips into the open gondola of a semitruck. Some of the trees were as thick as Gordon's waist when they were fed into the beast. But at the end of it all, they'd been reduced to chips the size of quarters. Gordon was watching me.

"I admit it," I shouted over the din, "I'm impressed. What's your point?"

"This isn't the only bay," Gordon yelled back. "There are two more just like it beyond this one. We've got nearly six hundred workers here, woodcutters, drivers, loaders, secretaries. We're one of the biggest employers in the county."

"I know that."

"Knowin' it's one thing. Seeing it's another. I just wanted you to get a close look at what you and your Mex pal are messing with. All those men down there owe their livelihoods to my family. We own 'em, like the trucks and the chippers."

I glanced around the plant floor. At a quick guess, there were two dozen men working at various tasks—hard hats, in jeans and flannel shirts. A few of them glanced up at me curiously, and I recognized a face or two, from school days or just seeing them around. One guy even waved.

"You catch my drift?" Gordon shouted.

"I think so," I said. "Shall we go?" I turned away without waiting for his answer, and went back through the double doors. I'd said I was impressed. And I was. I truly was.

23
LET'S MAKE A DEAL

"TEN THOUSAND," Ray said, rotating his coffee cup between his fingertips. We were at his table in the Nest. He'd arrived later than usual, and for a while I'd wondered if perhaps he'd flown off to Toronto after all. I wasn't sure how I felt about that—until he'd walked in the door.

"Fifteen thousand, actually," I said. "Don't forget my five."

"Okay, fifteen. What do you think of the offer?"

"What do you mean?"

"Exactly that. They made it to you, not me. What do you think of it?"

"If you're asking me if I could use five grand, the answer's yes. In my financial circles, that's not exactly chump change."

"Mine, either."

"Still, it's not much, considering how much might be at stake: the factory, the land, whatever. It must be worth multiple millions."

"I don't follow you. So they can afford fifteen grand. So what?"

"Owney mentioned he'd talked to his lawyers about you. Why would he do that unless he considered you some kind of a threat? Maybe, just maybe, because of the way he inherited the business, he thinks you might be entitled to whatever Jimmy's share of things should have been."

"For openers, I don't give a damn about their money. And anyway, legally, any claim I'd have would be pretty shaky. I mean, hell, at this point I can't even prove that . . . Jimmy's dead," he finished thoughtfully.

"That's right, you can't. And suddenly things look quite different, don't they?"

"Yeah." He nodded. "I thought I was looking for a ghost. It may be a lot simpler than that."

"Or it may not," I said. "The only thing that's really changed is that they're willing to hand over ten grand in nuisance money just to make you go away."

"Like an insurance company settling a lawsuit they don't want to bother with? That's not very flattering."

"Believe me, flattery was the last thing they had in mind. They um . . . gave me a quick tour of the plant afterward."

"The plant? Why?"

"To make the point that they have resources available, financial and otherwise, that you haven't."

"What's it like in there?"

"Big. Busy. Incredibly noisy. Basically, the place is a monster Cuisinart that eats whole trees at one end and spits out poker chips at the other."

He eyed me thoughtfully for a moment without speaking. "And?" he said at last.

"If you're wondering if it could make a body disappear, the answer is yes. That thing could probably solve the world's overpopulation problem overnight. But I'd also say it's unlikely Jimmy could have disappeared that way."

"Why?"

"People," I said simply. "The place is a beehive. You only saw part of the show last night. The inside is even worse. The plant's lit up like a night game and there were at least two dozen hard hats working on the line. I suppose you could bypass the safety gates and feed a . . . body into the machinery in a load of logs,

112

say. But the first part of the process is wide open. Any number of people could see it. Besides, if anything like that had actually happened, why would they show it to me?"

"I don't know. To discourage you? To prove to you that trying to find Jimmy is a lost cause?"

"If that's actually what happened to him, then finding him may *be* a lost cause."

"Maybe it is," he conceded. "But I don't think so. If it was, then why all the pressure? Why bother with the cable from Canada or to try to buy me off?"

"Does this mean you're not going to take the money?"

"Mitch, if they had anything to do with Jimmy's disappearance, if they even know anything about it and are holding back, then money isn't nearly enough to cover the debt. I'm sorry, I hope you weren't counting on the five thousand."

"Actually, I was. I was planning a big shop fest. A whole week at the mall."

"Somehow, you don't strike me as the shop-till-you-drop type."

"How little you know me."

"Sad but true," he said, with his first smile of the evening. "But it does give me something to look forward to. Getting to know you, I mean. And here's lesson one. You're holding out on me, holding something back. Are you taking pressure for helping me?"

"I um . . . yes," I admitted. "A little. Actually, more than a little. But it might have happened anyway, and I'm no better at knuckling under than you are. I can handle it."

"Are you sure?"

"Absolutely," I lied. "No problem."

24
STORM SIGNALS

OVER THE next few days, Ray drove into the hills every morning and returned at dusk, tired but not discouraged. I think he felt relieved to be doing *something*, whether it paid off or not. And in the evenings, we had dinner together. And we talked. And we became . . . friends, of a sort. But there was no chance we'd turn into buddies. The heat between us was already intense, and getting warmer.

I found myself thinking of him often, in the middle of paperwork, or driving, or whatever. And I also found myself taking a little extra time with my hair, and choosing what I wore a bit more carefully. I didn't suddenly start showing up for work in *Tammy and the Bachelor* frocks or trying out the latest *Cosmo* look, but I did spend an extra minute or two pawing through my closet looking for something decent to wear.

Of course, I never found anything that seemed remotely attractive, but I tried, and apparently it was worth it. Ray noticed things about me, new earrings, a peasant blouse, everything, really. And I was learning to read him a little, as well. His seemingly wooden stare masked a quirky, deadpan sense of humor. And I could also sense the shape our relationship might take, built on respect as well as chemistry. Neither of us tried to rush things—we weren't children, and we were both a bit battle wary—but something good was happening between us and we both knew it. We were friends and allies, who might well become lovers, in time. I was sure of it. But then too many things began to happen. Too fast.

I was in my office at the Nest, finishing up the paperwork on the dive shop's inventory. Hannah McClain rapped once, sharply, then stalked in.

"We need to talk," she said curtly, closing the door behind her. She was dressed for shopping, an ankle-length muted tweed skirt and jacket. Her makeup was immaculate, and I envied her. If I wear anything more complicated than lipstick and a trace of blush, I look like a hooker on Halloween. It must be a great comfort to know that first grim look in your morning mirror can be transmuted into Barbie perfection with a little effort.

But if marrying money had improved her clothes and her look, some things hadn't changed. She'd always been working-woman-direct with me. She still was.

"People tell me you and Ray Calderon are getting pretty tight," she said brusquely. "I understand you're together every night here, now. Have you two got something semiserious going on?"

I didn't say anything.

"Look, don't play coy with me, Mitch, I don't give a damn about your love life; whom you jump in the sack with is your business. The thing is, if you do care about Calderon at all, then you've got to get him to move on before he gets hurt."

"Why should he get hurt? What's going on?"

"It's . . . Owney," she said reluctantly, slumping down into the chair facing my desk. "Ever since Calderon's brother showed up, Owney's been coming unglued. He's acting sly, keeping things from me. We had a major confrontation about it last night, and he told me he'd been waiting for something like this to happen all his life."

"Something like what?"

"I'm not sure I understand it completely. Hell, I'm not sure

Freud would understand it. I suppose the heart of the matter is that Owney blames himself for his mom being crippled. He's convinced it's all his fault."

"I thought she was hurt in a fall or something, years ago."

"She was. He was seven when she got pregnant the second time, and surprise, surprise, he was jealous—afraid the new baby would take his place. He wanted it to go away, and even prayed it would. So when Audrey fell and miscarried, Owney thought his prayers had been answered, that he'd made it happen. And down deep, he's been terrified ever since that she'd find out somehow and stop loving him or disown him or whatever. Which may be why we've been married three years and still live with his mother and he won't even discuss having kids, or . . . God, what a mess." She pressed her fingertips against her temples, massaging them.

"Why are you telling me this?"

"Because I need your help, Mitch. You were always decent to me in school when a lot of kids treated me like white trash. I know everyone in town thinks I humped Owney into marrying me. Well, maybe I did. Nothing ever came easy for me. But I didn't marry him just for the money. And right now I'm willing to drop a fair chunk of cash to avoid trouble. How much would it take to get Calderon to back off? Just to go away?"

"I really couldn't say," I said carefully.

"Then I'll say. I can probably scrape together seven or eight thousand in cash if I sell some things Owney gave me. It'll have to be enough. It's not like he's actually entitled to anything, you know. His brother might have been, but Ray's not. Anyway, that's the best I can do."

"But why do anything? Why do you want him to go?"

"Because I'm afraid of what might happen if he stays. Owney's a wonderful guy in many ways. He's honest and generous and . . . But on this one subject, he's as crazy as his father must have been. And he's not the only one. Do you know Owney's uncle Gordon?"

"We've met. I don't know him well."

"Count your blessings. Gordon's a mess, a major screwup. He's been in trouble most of his life for bum checks, con games, stuff like that. Both Audrey and Owney's grandfather cut him off years ago, but he conned Owney into giving him another chance. Blood's thicker than water, that sort of thing. Owney got him a cushy job at the plant, made him head of security, which is probably appropriate, since I think Gordon probably knows a lot about theft. Audrey's tried to warn Owney about him, and I have, too, but he won't listen. Maybe he sees him as a father figure, I don't know. But Gordon's been working on him ever since, looking for an angle, a way to manipulate him. And Calderon's supplying the perfect opportunity."

"How do you mean?"

"I understand that Calderon's been nosing around up in the hills, checking things out. What's he doing up there, anyway?"

"That's really his business, isn't it?"

"Not anymore. Gordon's put the word out at the plant that Calderon's sizing up the McClain property, that he's getting ready for a lawsuit that'll throw everybody out of work."

"That's nonsense."

"Probably, but I think Owney's bought into it, and some of the mouth-breathers who do scut work at the plant have, too. And those boys can be dead serious when it comes to protecting their jobs. Mitch, you've got to call Calderon off, or he damned well might end up like his brother."

"What do you know about his brother?"

"Nothing. Only what I heard that first night. He went out to the plant, then came to the house, then apparently wound up in the river. The only part that strikes me as odd at all is that Audrey said Ross wasn't there."

"You mean he was?"

"He must have been. He almost never leaves the house, even on his days off. He's always sucking around Audrey, or me. God, I want to get out of that damned tomb and get a place of our own. But it'll never happen if Owney winds up in jail for getting your pal beaten half to death, or worse. So how about it? Can we make some kind of an arrangement?"

"You really don't know, do you?" I said.

"Know what?"

"That Owney already tried to buy Ray off. He offered him ten thousand just to go away. Ray turned it down."

"He offered him . . . ten thousand?" she said, paling beneath her makeup. "He um . . . no, he didn't tell me about it. It's Gordo. Damn him! He's got Owney's head so screwed up, he doesn't know what he's doing. And now he's cutting me out of the picture."

"Why would he do that?"

"Don't you get it, Mitch? If Owney racks up your pal and maybe winds up in jail, who do you think will end up running things around here? Audrey's getting shakier by the day, and I may be a McClain, but my prenup agreement keeps me completely out of the picture as far as the business is concerned. There's a lot at stake here, Mitch. Millions. You've got to get Calderon out of here. At least for a while."

"If it were up to me, he'd be gone already," I said honestly. "Not for your sake, for his. But it's not up to me. He won't go."

"Don't sell yourself short. You could talk him into it if you wanted to badly enough."

"What do you mean?"

"You know exactly what I mean, girlfriend. You could handle him the same way I landed Owney. We're not in high school anymore. You may not be drop-dead gorgeous, lady, but you're a handsome package, and you could be better if you worked at it. You can change Calderon's mind. And I can make it worth your while to try."

"Maybe you could," I conceded. "But I'm not quite ready to . . . how did you put it? Hump my way into a relationship? Look, I understand what you're trying to do, and I've got no problem with it, or with you. Unfortunately, I don't think Calderon's interested in money at the moment. All he really cares about is finding his brother, and I doubt he'll leave until he does."

"Then maybe he won't leave at all," she said coldly, rising to go. "Okay, I've tried to do my good deed for the day, Mitch. Now, maybe you'll do me a small favor in return. Tell Calderon if he's dead set on committing suicide to please take a header off the Mackinac Bridge. The view's terrific, and it'd be a lot less trouble for the rest of us. I'm . . . sorry about all this, Mitch. I'll see you."

She stalked out and I watched her thread her way through the lunch crowd. She even moved like a model, poised, polished, and prosperous. We had a lot in common, Hannah and I. Working-class roots and ambition, and probably other things, as well. But we'd chosen different routes to get where we were going. By most standards, she was well ahead of the game. She'd already acquired a husband and money and social position. But somehow I couldn't find it in my heart to envy her. Not even a little.

25
BABES AT SEA

AUDREY MCCLAIN moved very differently through the same room later that afternoon, gliding silently between the empty tables on a contraption that looked more like a hot rod than a wheelchair. Its frame was hot pink and its tires were a foot high and four inches wide, with knobby mud-runner treads. Audrey guided it as adroitly as a top-gun pilot, looking eagerly about as she fairly flew through the room, taking in the Nest as though she'd never seen anyplace quite so interesting. She was dressed for action, too, in an electric pink Liz Claiborne running suit that matched her chair, and high-top Nikes. Good God, her spine was a pretzel, her shoulders were so rigid that she had to bob her noggin about like a robin just to see where she was going, and yet she seemed more vital and alive than people half her age without a mark on 'em. It brightened my day just to see her. I rose from behind my desk and ambled out to meet her.

"Hi," I said. "Are you late for lunch or early for dinner?"

"Neither," she said. "I hope I'm right on time."

"For what?"

"Our date," she said mischievously. "You promised to take me sailing. Don't you remember?"

"I remember . . . that the subject came up. I don't recall setting a specific timetable."

"Ah, then perhaps it was your father who promised. People keep telling me I'm getting forgetful. Maybe they're right."

"Mrs. McClain, somehow I get the feeling you're no more forgetful than you find it convenient to be."

"My dear, you're much too young to be a cynic," she said, smiling. "I should be mortally offended by your mistrust, but I'll tell you what. Suppose I let you redeem yourself and your reprobate father at the same time. I had Ross drop my boat at the pier this morning. It's a gorgeous day, and from the looks of things, your business can spare you for an hour or so. Especially since you'll be honoring an old family promise. What do you say?"

"I'd say if you'd phoned ahead, I might have saved you a trip, Mrs. McClain. Hannah was already here."

"Hannah? Whatever for?"

"I think you know why she came, Mrs. McClain."

"Call me Audrey," she said irritably. "And you've lost me completely. In case you haven't gathered, our little clan isn't exactly *The Donna Reed Show*. We're more like the Borgias. Now what, exactly, did Hannah want?"

"She . . . asked me to buy off Ray Calderon somehow—to bribe him to leave town."

"Ah, it's Owney." She nodded. "She's worried about him. Well, perhaps she should be. He's always been high-strung, and lately . . . Still, I don't think Calderon is the problem, and for my part, I'd be very sorry to see him leave. He's made life more interesting than it's been in years. Everyone's in such an uproar. It's very exciting. Besides, without him, I might not have met you. Or had the courage to . . . come here."

"I don't understand. Why not?"

"Call it rust, for lack of a better word," she said brusquely. "People in my situation tend to limit our lives. So many things are difficult that over time we . . . give them up. Until one day we realize there's no reason to get out of bed. Nothing's left of our lives, or dreams. The funny thing is, from where I sit," she said, indicating her chair with a graceful wave of her hand, "I see it happen every day to people who aren't handicapped in any way. They do nothing and call it a lifestyle. Have you noticed?"

"Yes." I nodded. "I suppose that's true."

"So sometimes we need a healthy dose of trouble to remind us that life's a gamble but we're still in the game. So suppose we break out of our ruts together and just sail away for an hour or two. What do you say?"

"I'd say you missed your calling," I said. "You should have been a salesperson."

"Why? Have I made a sale?"

"Absolutely. Red!" I called. "I'm bailing out for a while. Catch for me, okay?" Red yelled something semi-intelligible from the kitchen, probably obscene. I followed Mrs. McClain and her racing chair off the back-deck ramp down to the pier.

Most people consider Labor Day the end of the sailing season, so most of the berths along the pier were empty. The few craft left in the water were shrouded and silent, orphans awaiting one last harried visit by their owners for a final housecleaning before being beached and stored for the winter. Their owners don't know what they're missing. Autumn's the best sailing season of all.

True, October winds are notoriously unstable on the big lakes. They roar in from nowhere, growing from zephyr to gale force in a matter of hours, sometimes less. TV weathermen shake their heads and make happy talk over their multicolored maps and satellite photos. And every year, a few unlucky souls miss a small-craft warning or make some other minor, fatal mistake. And boats and boaters drift down through the dark, storm-roiled water to sleep with the *Edmund Fitzgerald* and the six thousand other hulks already at rest on the lake bed.

But today looked safe enough. The breeze was crisp and cool, eight knots and steady, with no changes expected. The lake glittered like a vast millpond dusted with diamonds in the early-afternoon sun.

Mrs. McClain's sailer was a twenty-eight-foot catboat, a hardy little craft with a single sail, a lazy man's rig, easy to handle and very forgiving. The low lines give you a wonderful sense of being just a foot or so above the water. *"Kalevala?"* I said, reading the name on her stern.

"It's Finnish," Audrey said. "It means 'hero's dwelling place.' This was Owen's boat originally. She's been stored for years, but Owney had her refitted last spring. Ross tried to teach him to sail, but Owney's prone to motion sickness. A pity. His father was quite a hand at it."

"How um . . . how would you like to board her?" I asked.

"Could you pick me up? I'm really not very heavy."

"I think so." I slid one arm beneath her thighs and the other around her back and lifted her out of her chair. She weighed scarcely more than a child. I stepped carefully into the boat and lowered Audrey onto the stern seat. She fretted impatiently, eyes alight, as I took a few minutes to familiarize myself with the boat's rigging.

Satisfied, I checked the fuel for the inboard motor then fired it up and and we pooted out of the harbor under our own steam.

Catboats are civilized little motor sailers, but the breeze was fresh, so I shut her down as soon as we cleared the harbor mouth, then raised the mainsail and let the wind carry us out into the bay.

I tacked to the north, across and into the wind by turns, beginning a long circle that would give us an hour or two on the water, and a tailwind to chase us home if need be. I guessed Audrey would probably be game to ride out a hurricane, but courage can be a character flaw when you're dealing with wind or water.

"Are you a golf-type sailor?" she asked.

"Golf?"

"You know, all quiet on the putting green? Owen always preferred to sail in silence, and Ross never talks much, in any case. Is it all right to chat?"

"Sure. I always thought the best part of sailing was letting your hair down and telling fibs with no one to hear but the wind."

"Good. You first. I knew your father, and I remember you as a scrawny teenager a dozen years or so ago. And now you're back. From where? What have you been doing all this time?"

"Scraping by," I said. I tried to give her a nutshell version of my life as a working single mother, but she showed such persistent, genuine interest that I unwound more than I'd meant to. About how hard it was to leave Corey in a boarding school, and the paranoia of working with male divers on the platforms; having to second-guess every piece of advice, never sure if the advice was designed to help me or to jam me up, to prove a woman couldn't handle the job.

"It sounds awfully grim," Audrey said.

"It really wasn't. I liked the work, and most of the men were fine. But the constant . . . uncertainty got to me after a while. On the other hand, Lincoln freed the slaves. I could have left anytime."

"You mean you could have *quit* anytime," she said, "which isn't quite the same thing."

"Possibly not," I agreed. "On the other hand, you've had a plateful of troubles in your life, and I don't see you giving up."

"When you lose most of your . . . options, maybe you hang on tighter to those you have left. Like you, I was a single mother. After my accident, I had Owney to look after, and with Owen gone and my father-in-law in failing health, I was forced to become a competent businesswoman. There was simply no one else. Now that Owney's of age, I've backed away from actively running the family enterprises. I miss it sometimes, but then there are a good many things I miss. Being out on the water, for instance."

"Sailing? But you could do this anytime. You said Ross dropped the boat at the harbor, so I take it he sails."

"Ross has any number of talents," she said with a wry smile. "He's a good listener, for instance, but not much of a conversationalist. Besides, sailing is a little like love, I think. It loses some of the fun when it's paid for. Not that either of us know much about paying for love, I hope."

"Lady, I don't don't know much about love, paid for or any other kind. But I gather you do. People say you and Owen were an ideal couple."

"I suppose we seemed like it. God knows, he was a gorgeous man. Handsome as a male model . . ." Her voice trailed away.

"What is it?" I asked.

"Nothing. Only . . . this trouble over young Calderon seems to have brought those years back somehow. It all seems fresh again, as though it happened yesterday. You think the past is over and done with, that you've armored yourself against the pain of it. But memories are . . . very patient. They lie in wait. And when something calls them up, they're as savage and hurtful as when they were new. Things that happened years ago are clearer and stronger than yesterday."

"What kinds of things?"

"It's hard to explain," she said, as much to herself as to me. "I just have this dreadful feeling that . . . something is turning. Some great wheel, bringing it all back. The last time, I lost my love, and my . . . legs. And this time, I'll lose everything. Everything." Her eyes were on the horizon, although seeing into a distance I could only imagine. And my blood chilled with an atavistic reaction. She had spoken prophecy, like a Cassandra. Or Ashtoreth. She sensed an evil coming. And we both knew it was true, the way she-wolves scent danger when smoke is on the wind, though they've never seen fire.

"I'm sorry," she said. "I must sound certifiably senile to you."

"No," I said, more shaken than I cared to admit. "Sometimes people have . . . feelings they can't explain. And sometimes they're right."

"But more often they're wrong, my dear," she said with a

125

flicker of her usual smile. "Otherwise, Vegas and Atlantic City would be ghost towns."

"I don't understand. What do you mean when you said things are coming back?"

"Oh, memories are resurfacing, I suppose. I have a few, you know. First love. And sex. I remember every delicious bit of that. It all ended so soon, but . . ." Her voice trailed off again. I glanced at her. Her eyes were misty and her lip was trembling.

"Mrs. McClain? Audrey? If you'd rather we talked about something else . . ."

She swiveled slowly, tilting her head up at that odd angle, meeting my eyes. "Do you believe in ghosts?" she said quietly. "Do you believe . . . people—dead people—come back?"

"I don't know. Do you?"

"No," she said, shaking her head slowly. "No. Of course not. What a question." She didn't speak for a while after that, and I sensed she was collecting herself.

"I'm sorry," she said at last. "I do tend to ramble, don't I? And it's too fine a day for it."

"Maybe a sunny day's the best time to talk about ghosts," I suggested.

"No," she said briskly. "Talking about your problems is greatly overrated, I think. Let's talk shop, instead. How's your new business doing?"

"It could be better," I said, watching her to gauge her reaction. "I'm still learning."

"Glad to hear it. Most of the world's troubles are caused by people with more answers than questions. But for the record, if you ever need any help—advice, money, whatever—please come to me. Advice is free, and frankly I have more money than I know what to do with. I'll be disappointed if you don't ask."

And for a moment, I considered it. But only for a moment. If there was a door opening here, it wasn't one I cared to go through. "Didn't you say something a minute ago about sailing losing its fun if it's paid for?" I said.

126

"I'm not trying to buy your friendship, Mitch. Do you think so little of me?"

"What I think is, sailing and business are a lousy mix," I said, eyeing the sails critically. "And right now, we're sailing. Get ready to duck; we're going to come about."

"You're not turning back because of something I said?"

"Not at all. We've been beating into the wind since we left the harbor. I'm going to swing around to the southwest along the shoreline and run with it for a while."

"Good idea," she said, cocking her head to glance up at me mischievously. "The colors in the hills are lovely. I hope your Mr. Calderon's enjoying them."

I thrust the tiller over a bit more sharply than I'd intended. She ducked in plenty of time as the boom came across. The *Kalevala* heeled over smartly, wheeling like a quarterhorse on a fast track, immediately gaining way on her new tack as her sails filled. And we were off again, dancing over the water on canvas wings. The wind was rising a bit, nibbling at the crests of the waves.

We didn't talk for a while. I was busy steadying the *Kalevala* on her new heading and Audrey seemed content to enjoy the day, the light on the water, the autumn colors in the hills.

"What color is Mr. Calderon's car?" she asked. "Is it red?"

"Yes," I said. "A rental Escort. Why?"

"I thought I glimpsed a red car, a small one, for a moment back there."

"Where?"

"Somewhere near the crest of that hill, I think. I can't see it now. . . ."

She flinched as a gout of water suddenly erupted a few yards off our port side.

"What—" Her voice was drowned by the echo of gunfire from the shore. Another spout erupted just ahead of us; then a third slug slammed into the *Kalevala*'s hull, exploding a gout of splinters and water only a few feet from Audrey.

26

SNIPER

"GET DOWN!" I roared.

I grabbed her wrist, yanked her to me, then slid us both down into the bottom of the boat, realizing even as I did it that it didn't offer a damned bit of protection. There was already an ugly hole just above the waterline where the slug had punched through the hull, and we were taking on water with every wave. If we foundered out here, we'd be sitting ducks. Assuming we didn't drown first.

I pulled the rudder over, filling the sails, running the *Kalevala* slightly off the wind. I nosed her sharply out into the bay while desperately trying to avoid losing headway. A few minutes before, I'd been marveling at how easily she handled, dancing over the waves like a ballerina. Now she was pure pigboat, leaden-hulled, plowing through the water like a gut-shot whale.

Still, we were moving offshore and the shooting seemed to have stopped for the moment. I peered over the rail, searching the shoreline first, then higher into the hills, looking for the gunman, movement, anything. Nothing. No people, no vehicles. I caught a hazy glimpse of something on a bluff well back in the hills, but it seemed to be climbing, rising into the trees. And then it faded altogether. Smoke? Powder smoke, maybe? I tried to fix in my memory the area where I'd seen it.

One thing was certain, though: Whoever'd been shooting at us was pretty fair at it. We'd been at least two hundred yards offshore, and the firing hadn't come from the beach, or I would have seen the flashes. If it came from the bluff where I'd spotted the smoke, the distance was probably closer to three hundred yards. Yet we'd been hit. One helluva shot. But there was something wrong about it. Something about the sound . . .

"Can I get up, please?" Audrey said quietly. "I think I'd rather be shot than have you strangle me to death." She was right. My arm was clamped around her narrow shoulders in a choke hold that would have done a TV wrestler proud.

"Sorry," I said, releasing her. "Are you all right?"

"I think so," she said. "I don't have much feeling below my waist anyway, but I don't seem to be wounded or anything. And you?"

"I'm okay. A little shaky." I helped her back up on the stern seat. She was shivering uncontrollably. The water sloshing in the bottom of the *Kalevala* had soaked us both. "Here," I said, "you'd better take my jacket."

"No. You're as wet as I am."

"I'm used to it," I said. "I get wet for a living, remember? Take it, please."

"Thank you," she said gratefully as I slipped it over her shoulders. "My God, was someone shooting at us?"

"Looks like it," I said, indicating the ugly hole forward. "Didn't miss by much, either. Are you sure you're all right?"

"I'm fine, dear, just a little bruised. That was a very brave thing you did, shielding me."

"It was just a reflex," I said, my voice sounding a bit unsteady in my own ears. I took a deep, ragged breath, and realized my hands were trembling. I glanced around, taking stock of our situation. We were well out into the bay now, three-quarters of a mile offshore and probably five or six miles south of the harbor.

129

"It was still a brave thing to do, and I won't forget it."

"Audrey, it's the least of our problems now. What the hell's going on here? Who'd be shooting at you?"

"At me? No one. Why do you think the shots were aimed at me?"

"It's your boat."

"Actually, it's Owney's boat, though Ross probably uses it more."

"Who knew we were out here?"

"It was no secret. Why should it be? My family knew, of course, and Ross. Why?"

"I'm just trying to figure out how much trouble we're in. Whether whoever was shooting at us might try again. There are a few spots along the shore where we could put in and get to a phone, but if someone's stalking us, I want a lot of people around when we land. I think we'd better make for the harbor."

"We don't have to land to telephone," she said. "We keep a portable phone aboard for emergencies. It's in a bag in the forward locker."

"I'll get it," I said. "Can you manage the helm?"

"Of course," she said. "I'm not helpless, you know. The phone's in the zipper pocket on the side of the bag."

I made my way forward, keeping a wary eye on the boom, an old habit when sailing with a stranger. I found the bag and the phone, dialed 911, and gave the operator a quick rundown of our situation. Naturally, she put me on hold.

But only for a moment. There was some crackling static and then Charlie Bauer came on. From the background noise, I guessed he was speaking from a prowl car.

"Mitch, are you and Audrey all right? We had a report that someone took a shot at you."

"We're fine, considering. The boat's not, though. We're holed near the waterline."

"Are you sinking?"

"No, but we're taking on water. I can make the harbor all right, but I'd feel better if you could get Mrs. McClain off."

"I'm pulling into the harbor now. We'll have the patrol boat under way in a couple of minutes. Where are you exactly?"

"About five miles due south of the harbor. We're a sailboat, Charlie, the only one in sight. Even a lubber like you ought to be able to spot us."

"Good. If you're barking at me, you can't be hurt too badly. I've gotta go. Give me your number; I'll call you back as soon as we're under way."

I read it to him and he hung up. I stuffed the phone back into the bag and carried it with me back to the stern. Audrey'd held our heading well enough, but I noticed she was hunching over the tiller and her color looked a little ashen to me.

"Help's on the way," I said, taking the helm. "How are you doing?"

"I'm fine," she said. "Give me the bag, please." She unzipped the center pocket and rummaged through enough medication to stock a small clinic. She found the bottle she wanted, shook out a couple of horse-sized pills, and popped them in her mouth. Then she reached over the side and scooped up a palmful of lake water and washed them down.

"I ah . . . I feel a little unsteady," she said. "May I . . . lean on you?" She slumped over against me and I barely caught her in time to keep her from sliding off the seat. She was shivering fiercely, her lips blue. I pulled her as close to me as I could and wrapped my free arm around her. After a few minutes, her trembling eased a bit and her breathing steadied. And so did mine.

The phone in the seabag rang with a muffled burble. I ignored it. I could already see the patrol boat roaring out of the harbor mouth, heading directly toward us.

27
THE RESCUE

IT TOOK the patrol boat less than fifteen minutes to cover the open water between us. The pilot, one of Charlie's deputies, Bo Unger, eased back his throttle while he was thirty yards off so that his bow wave wouldn't rock us too badly, then eased his craft alongside. I'd already given Audrey the tiller and dropped *Kalevala*'s sail.

"Mitch?" Charlie yelled. "Are you two okay?"

"I'm fine. Audrey's a little shaken, though. You'd better take her aboard and get her ashore."

I tossed him a line as he timed the rise and fall of the boats and then stepped across the interval with surprising grace. Charlie's not neurotic about his dislike of deep water, but I know he's happier with solid ground under him. Preferably a mountain.

"Mrs. McClain," he said gently, kneeling beside Audrey, "if you don't mind, I'm going to have to manhandle you a bit, okay?" He picked her up as gently as a babe, stepped over to the patrol boat, and placed her carefully down on the stern seat. Unger brought her a blanket and the two men made her as comfortable as possible. Charlie spoke to her for a moment and she nodded, then he vaulted back aboard the *Kalevala*.

"Now tell me about the shooting," he said quietly. "Is there any chance it might have been accidental? It's hunting season, you know."

"No way, Charlie. We were a good two hundred yards off-shore and there were several shots. One of them holed our bow. . . ." I hesitated.

"What is it?"

"There was something about the shots that bothered me, and I just realized what it was. The sound. At that distance, it could-n't have been a shotgun, but I don't think it was a rifle, either. I think it may have been a handgun."

"How could you tell the difference that far off?"

"I was raised around guns, Charlie. My dad taught me to shoot when I was fourteen. I'm no expert, but I definitely know one from another. This gun sounded more like a bark than a crack, you know? I fairly sure it was a handgun."

"At two hundred yards?" he said doubtfully.

"All of that, maybe more. I think I can show you the place."

"Later. I want to get Mrs. McClain ashore. I don't like her color. Come on aboard; we'll take this boat in tow."

"No, you'd better go ahead and let me follow in the *Kalevala*. She's fine on her own, but if you try towing her, she may ship enough water to swamp."

"Are you sure she's safe to sail?"

"She's fine. The hull's fiberglass, so the hole shouldn't get any worse. In fact, if you want, you can send Audrey on in with Unger and I'll take you back to pinpoint the area the shots came from while it's still fresh in my mind."

He eyed me doubtfully for a moment, then nodded. "Fair enough. Bo! Head on in and see to Mrs. McClain. Mitch is going to show me where the shooting came from. You tell Nance to listen for my call, and I'll vector him into the area if I can."

"Yes, sir." Unger wheeled the patrol boat slowly around, then putted it away from us for twenty yards or so, getting clear. I waved good-bye to Audrey and she lifted her hand vaguely in reply. Then Unger revved up the patrol boat and roared off, headed for the harbor.

Charlie gingerly took a seat in the stern and held the tiller while I raised the *Kalevala*'s sail again. Then I parked beside him, took the helm, and swung her around. I headed back toward the hills on a heading that kept us well offshore. I doubted the gunman was still there, but why tempt fate?

"What the hell's going on around here, Charlie?" I said. "Why on earth would anyone take potshots at us?"

"You tell me. Anybody mad at you, Mitch?"

"Me? Nobody. Besides, the slug hit closer to Audrey, and it's her boat, or her family's, anyway. She mentioned that Ross sails it sometimes. Know anybody who's mad at Ross?"

"Not offhand. How far are we from the spot?"

"Six or seven minutes, maybe less."

"Okay, don't rock this thing. I want to take a look at the hole and I'm not real steady on my pins in boats." He made his way forward, crouched, step by cautious step, graceless as a dancing bear. He knelt by the hole, examined it carefully, then swiveled around and ran his fingertips over the opposite side of the boat. "Gotcha," he said with a nod.

"Got what?"

"The slug is buried in the starboard here. Hell of an entrance hole. Looks like a fairly large caliber. Funny angle to it, though. Were you heeled over when the shooting started?"

"Heeled over? No, we were just scuffin' along, talking. Why?"

"I'll have to check it with a rod to be sure, but the hole and the slug seem to be almost directly opposite each other at roughly the same height. The shots must have come from the beach, Mitch."

"They couldn't have. The beach was clear, Charlie. We would have seen the shooter."

"Could he have been under cover?"

"I don't see how. It's just ahead. Take a look for yourself. The beach is clear, more or less. There's nowhere to hide, and even if he was concealed, I would have seen his smoke. See that cleft in the hills? Over there? With all the cedars on it? We were roughly opposite that spot when the shooting started. And just above it to the south? The small bluff? That's where I think I spotted powder smoke rising."

"How certain are you?"

"Not completely," I said. "I was kind of busy at the time."

"Yeah, I expect you were. How far offshore were you when you got hit?"

"Probably a hundred yards closer than we are now. If it's all the same, I'll keep her out here. For all we know, somebody's got a grudge against catboats."

"Not likely," he said, making his way gingerly back to the stern and taking his seat. "But for what it's worth, there's a road just beyond that bluff you pointed out. The shooter could've been up there, Mitch, but I don't see how he could have used a handgun. Even if you were a lot closer to the beach, it'd still be nearly a two-hundred-yard shot. I couldn't hit a barn at that distance with a pistol, and I don't know many people who could."

"I didn't say it was a pistol, I just said it sounded like one."

"Well, whatever it was, it worked pretty good, from the looks of that hole up front."

"Forward," I said automatically.

"Yeah, right," he said dryly. He took a small cellular handset from a clip on his belt. "Nance? Can you read me?"

I could only hear static, but apparently it made sense to Charlie. "I want you to get on the old logging track that follows the lakeshore up in the hills. Take the first left, then a left again. About halfway up, you're gonna pass an area where you can see the lake. A bluff. Check it out, see what you can turn up. Get back to me. Copy?"

More static. "Roger," Charlie said. "We'll be back at the harbor in . . ." He arched an eyebrow at me.

"Half an hour," I said.

"Half an hour," he echoed. "Yeah. Hold him there. Don't talk to him or let him talk to anyone else unless he asks for an attorney. Out." Charlie stuck the radio back in the case on his belt.

"Hold whom where?" I asked.

"A suspect. Nance picked him up right after you called."

"Who?"

"A guy who was in the vicinity."

"Just a guy? Let me guess. He was in the hills and he was driving a red Ford Escort, right? Don't tell me Nance arrested Calderon."

"He's not under arrest, just detained. Why? Do you think he might have done it?"

"No, of course not."

"Then why did you guess we'd picked him up?"

"Because if it had been anyone else, you'd have given me a straight answer instead of waltzing me around. And it just dawned on me that when I called nine-one-one, they patched me straight through to you and you said you'd already had a report about the shooting. But since it's small-game season and gunfire in the hills is normal this time of year, nobody would bother reporting it. So what did your caller report?"

"He said a guy matching Calderon's description was shooting at a boat."

I angled the bow a bit to the north to catch a better angle on the wind, using the moment to consider the possibilities.

"Well?" Charlie said.

"Who was the caller?"

"Didn't identify himself. In fact, he didn't call nine-one-one direct, he called city hall and they relayed the message to us."

"City hall? Why city hall?"

"I don't know. Maybe he was excited and misread the directory."

"No," I said. "I don't think he made a mistake. He knew exactly what he was doing. He must have."

"What do you mean?"

"Charlie, I was a hundred and fifty, maybe two hundred yards away from whoever was shooting, and I couldn't see anyone. How could your witness see them? We were the only boat in the bay and there are no houses nearby."

"Maybe they were closer than you were. A hunter, or maybe somebody just taking in the colors."

"Right, a hunter or a tourist who was packing a phone? And knew the number for city hall, too? There aren't any phone booths in those hills, and if your caller reported the shooting before I did, he didn't have time to make it to town. I think he made the call right after he finished shooting at us."

"I don't follow you," Charlie said, looking off toward the shoreline, thinking. "Why would the shooter call in? And why call city hall instead of nine-one-one?"

"Aren't all nine-one-one calls taped?"

"Yes," Charlie admitted, "but how would your phantom caller know that?"

"Come on, Charlie. Anyone who's ever watched a cop show on TV knows that. This thing has to be some kind of a setup and you know it."

"No, I don't know it. Who's being set up?"

"Calderon, obviously. He's the one who got caught."

"Set up by whom? Don't tell me you're buying into this obsession of his about the McClain family?"

"Obsession? Is that what you think it is?"

"Possibly. Look, I've seen this kind of thing before, Mitch. Somebody dies or gets killed, and the ones left behind are hurting and angry. They need to hit back at something; to blame somebody for what happened. Sometimes they take it out on the cops. Say it's our fault the road wasn't properly lighted, or ask why the hell we didn't lock up Uncle Charlie before he got drunk and wrapped his Chevy around a tree at a hundred and forty."

"Does Calderon seem like the hysterical type to you?"

"No, but his brother's disappeared, maybe drowned—hell, we don't even know what happened to him. It's natural for him to want to blame somebody for it. So he comes up with the idea that Owen McClain or his family may be responsible for what happened to Jimmy. He starts wandering around the hills on his cockamamie manhunt, and then he sees Audrey out here . . . and maybe he decides to even the score a little."

"You can't really believe that."

"I don't know what I believe yet. But right now, we've got a witness who said he saw him do it, and he's got a semicredible motive. It's at least a possibility, Mitch. Maybe you're just too . . . close to the problem to see it."

"Too close? What's that supposed to mean? That I'm blinded by hormones? Something like that?"

"I didn't mean that, exactly. But you've been spending a lot of time with the guy, and I've noticed you seem . . . attracted to him. So maybe you're not exactly a neutral observer here. On the other hand, I'm not sure I am, either."

"Why not?"

"For the same reason. Because you're apparently attracted to the guy, okay? Enough said? Or do I have to spell it out?"

"My God, Charlie," I said, "you can't mean you're jealous. We're friends, for God's sake."

"That's right, we are. So speaking as a friend, it bothers me that you barely know Calderon and yet you seem to be backing him all the way. I don't know what's going on here, but what I do know is that since Calderon came to town we've had non-stop problems, and now somebody's using you and Audrey McClain for target practice, and I don't like it. I don't like any of it."

"I don't like being a target, either, but I don't think the shots had anything to do with me. I just happened to be there."

"If that hole up there was a foot or two closer, whom it was meant for'd be a moot point. And if you weren't the target, then Audrey must have been. And damn it, Mitch, I can't think of a soul who's got a beef with Audrey McClain, except maybe your new pal. Can you?"

"No, but if whoever did it meant to run Calderon off, you're reacting right on cue."

"Same question: Who'd want me to run him off?"

"What about that navy cop? It's exactly what he wanted you to do, wasn't it?"

"He's gone. Checked out of his motel yesterday and caught a flight south."

138

"Did he? Did you see him get on the plane?"

"I didn't actually buckle him into his seat," Charlie admitted, exasperated. "I didn't figure I had to. He may be a jerk, Mitch, but he's also a cop. I can't see him shooting up the countryside. Besides, he wouldn't have known you were out here. Any other candidates? Other than Owen's ghost, I mean."

"Why do you say ghost?"

"Because that's what Calderon's chasing up here. The hell of it is, I think he's got you half-believing it, too."

"I may not be the only one, Charlie. Audrey McClain asked me earlier if I believed in ghosts. And I think she was serious. She seemed genuinely troubled by something."

"Terrific. So what are we doing out here? Why not call Ghostbusters?"

"Because ghosts don't need guns; they scare people to death. I'm just wondering why she asked."

"I don't know, and right now I haven't time to worry about it. I've got a plateful of questions and zero answers, so let's get this tub back to the harbor and try to find a few, okay? One thing, though. If I was out of line for worrying about you and Calderon, I apologize."

"I'm not offended, Charlie. I'm just . . . surprised. To be honest, I'm not sure how I feel about it. And I think I'll wait until people stop shooting at me to figure it out."

He nodded. "Good idea. Besides, if they shoot a little straighter next time, they may solve the problem for us."

"You've got a weird sense of humor, Charlie."

"Who said I was kidding?" he grumbled.

28
ON THE BEACH

꩜

THE HARBOR was a mob scene when I nosed the *Kalevala* into her berth. Two prowl cars were parked near the patrol boat's berth. One was a county car, with Tim Nance at the wheel and Ray Calderon in the backseat. The other was a McClain Industrial Fuels silver-and-black security force car parked nearby, its multicolored strobe lights flashing like a jukebox on amphetamines. To my surprise, Audrey McClain was still there, huddled in her wheelchair on the Crow's Nest dining deck, wrapped in a shawl. Her color looked better than when I'd seen her last, but she still looked ashen and ill, gaunt as a death-camp survivor.

Owney was kneeling beside her chair, but he rose and stalked angrily down the dock toward us as soon as we neared the pier.

"Nice you could drop by, Charlie," he snapped as we moored the *Kalevala* into her berth. "What the hell were you doing out there, sight-seeing? Nance has already got Calderon under arrest. And you, Mitchell, what in the world were you thinking of, taking my mother out on the bay? She could have been killed!"

"Lighten up, Mr. McClain," Charlie said mildly. "Mitch had no way of knowing there'd be trouble. She just took Audrey for a little sail on a calm day, at your mother's request, as I understand it. Seems to me if you've got a problem with that, you ought to take it up with Audrey."

"I'm taking it up with you, Bauer, and Mitch, too. Damn it, everyone knows my mother is getting on and her judgment's shaky. But if you're figuring on taking advantage of that, Mitch, you can forget it. I make the financial decisions for the family now. You won't gain anything by sucking up to her, so do yourself a favor and stay away from my mother. All she can buy for you is trouble."

It was a very near thing. Owney was standing at the edge of the pier, less than a foot from the water. And it took every ounce of won't-power I had to keep from grabbing him by the lapels of his perfectly tailored suit and pitching him headfirst into the harbor. I didn't, but the urge was so strong, I could almost see him arching like a diver into the oily murk. Charlie was eyeing me, concerned. I shook my head slowly. If there was going to be more trouble, I wouldn't be the cause of it. Besides, Owney outweighed me by at least a hundred pounds, and he'd been a pretty fair athlete once. Maybe we'd both get wet. And guess who'd get sued for assault?

But for a moment, just a moment, it was almost worth it.

"Owney," I said as civilly as I could manage, "I happen to like your mother very much, and I wouldn't dream of trying to take advantage of her. If you think you can run her life, take your best shot. From what I've seen of her, she can probably handle anything you can dish out. But don't try to order me around. I'm not on your payroll."

"Maybe not, but a lot of people in this town are, Mitch. It's tough for anyone in business to make it nowadays. And you're going to find out just how tough it can be."

"Come on, Mr. McClain, I know you're upset, and rightly so," Charlie interrupted, clapping an apparently friendly hand on Owney's shoulder and turning him away from the water and from me. "There's no need to threaten Mitch. Her business is small potatoes compared with yours, and yours must be doing

141

pretty well. That company security car looks brand new."

"We've had to take some extra precautions lately," Owney said grudgingly as Charlie led him off. I trailed a few paces behind. "We've bought some equipment and added a few men."

"Any particular reason?"

"Just some . . . trouble with trespassers."

"I don't recall any reports on it," Charlie said. "When was this?"

"Over the past few months. My uncle didn't want to bother you about it, and it was time we professionalized our security force anyway."

"I'm disappointed no one called us. If I'd known you were having problems out there, we could have increased our patrols in the area. And if security's a problem, a permanent installation—an electric fence or surveillance cameras—would be a lot more cost-effective than adding people. Especially the people you've been adding."

"Meaning what?"

"Meaning some of the people your uncle's been hiring out there have records, Owney. They're more apt to be security problems than solutions."

"If you were better at your job, Bauer, we wouldn't need a security force at all. And whom I hire at the plant is my business, not yours."

"Yes, sir, it certainly is. I just hope it stays that way," Charlie said mildly. "Excuse me a moment." He trudged over toward the McClain security car, leaving Owney alone on the dock. Neatly done. I stayed with Charlie. The last thing I wanted was more trouble with Owney. I really wanted to talk to Ray, but I doubted Tim Nance would let me. He'd stepped out of his prowl car and was waving spectators off with his baton.

Gordon McClain was talking quietly with a couple of hard hats from the plant when Charlie tapped him on the shoulder. "Hello, Gordo. Nice uniform. Almost looks official."

"Sheriff." Gordon McClain nodded warily as his friends

moved off. "I brought a few men along as backup, in case there was more trouble."

"There's no trouble here we can't handle," Charlie said. "How did you hear about it so quickly?"

"We monitor police band and nine-one-one calls. Just to be on the safe side."

"Yeah, I'll just bet you do. You wanna turn off the flashers on your prowl car, please? This isn't an emergency situation and we don't need to attract any more gawkers down here."

"If that Mex shooting at my sister-in-law isn't an emergency, then what is?" Gordon said.

"I didn't say the shooting wasn't serious. I said to turn off those flashers. Now do it." Charlie hadn't raised his voice, but there was no mistaking his tone. Gordon McClain hesitated a moment, meeting Charlie's stare. The two men were of a size, Charlie a little taller, Gordon a lot heavier. If push came to shove, I'd bet on Charlie anytime, if his sense of fair play didn't do him in.

"Hemmerli," McClain said without looking away. "Turn off your flashers. They bother the sheriff here."

The driver of the plant security car switched off the emergency lights, then eased his lanky frame out of the vehicle to eye Charlie across its roof. Charlie met his stare for a moment, then reached down and lifted the flap of Gordon's holster. It held a portable phone.

"A cellular thirty-eight." Gordon smirked, drawing it, offering it to Charlie. "Want to make a call?"

"Nah, since we're both here, I'll just give you the message personally," Bauer said evenly. "Ex-cons are legally barred from carrying weapons, security job or no security job. If I catch you with one, you're gonna need that phone to call a lawyer from the county lockup. And I don't like you wearing that holster, either, no matter what you've got in it."

"We're working on having that conviction expunged," Gordon said, flushing. "And meanwhile, what I carry in my holster—"

143

"Bothers me," Charlie said, cutting him off. "I don't like seeing ex-cons in uniform, even if they're only rent-a-cops. It demeans my profession and muddies up my day. And I *really* don't like having to wonder what you're packing in your holster, Gordo. So from now on, you'd best leave that gun belt behind when you're off company property. Because if you don't, I'm gonna have to satisfy my curiosity about it every five minutes or so. And don't use those emergency flashers off company property, either. You've got no legal authority. You're not cops."

"Maybe we should be," Gordon said. "If we were, riffraff like Calderon wouldn't be running around shooting at people."

"Mr. Calderon's here as a possible witness, and that's all," Charlie said. "He hasn't been charged with anything. So why don't you take your fancy prowl car and your new uniforms back to the plant to take care of all those security problems I hear you're having."

McClain stood his ground for a moment, then stalked angrily over to his prowl car. He yanked the door open, then turned back to Charlie. "Look, I know most cops figure a man's mistakes brand him for life, Bauer, but I'm all paid up for mine. Once my record's expunged, I'll by God expect to be treated like any other citizen."

"Don't worry, Gordo, if you manage to get your record erased, I'll know exactly how to treat you. The trouble with expungements is that they only fix the paperwork. They don't do a damned thing about my memory. Now move this prowl car off the beach before I cite it as a public nuisance."

McClain climbed into the car and slammed the door. Hemmerli shrugged and climbed in, then fired it up and backed slowly off the beach and into the Crow's Nest parking lot. He stopped there with the engine idling. The shirtsleeved shop rats who'd been talking to Gordon earlier joined them at the car, eyeing Charlie with open suspicion.

If it bothered Charlie, he didn't show it. We walked to the county prowl car. He huddled with Tim Nance a moment, then sent him off to clear the crowd. He opened the back door and gestured for Ray to step out.

"Mr. Calderon," Charlie said, shaking his head. "Seems like whenever I've got trouble lately, you're in the middle of it."

"I'm not in the middle of anything. I was just having a walk in the country when your deputy picked me up and hauled me down here."

"I see. Where were you exactly?"

"My car was parked on a turnout about halfway up Hill Road. I was wandering around a little way from it."

"You hear any shots while you were . . . wandering?"

"I heard shots," Ray acknowledged. "But I hear 'em fairly often up there. It's hunting season, isn't it?"

"That's right. Hunting, were you?"

"Nope, just hiking."

"So you weren't carrying a gun? Do you own a gun, Mr. Calderon?"

"Sure, I own several. They're all legally registered. And they're all back home in Virginia."

"You didn't bring one with you?"

"Sheriff, I flew here, remember? You can't carry weapons on a plane, and I had no reason to bring one. I'm no hunter."

"Or at least not for small game," Charlie said. "Where were you when you heard the shots?"

"In the woods, a hundred yards or so off the road. That's really all I can tell you. I don't know the area well enough to be certain of where I was, or where the shots came from."

"Understandable." Charlie nodded. "It's pretty wild country up there. How many shots did you hear?"

"There were . . . three or four, I believe. I really wasn't paying much attention."

"Three or four. Anything else?"

"Afraid not. Except that I thought they might have been from a handgun, which struck me as odd. A guy'd have to be a helluva shot to pop small game with a handgun."

145

"Whoever did the shooting was a helluva shot," Charlie said. "How good a shot are you, Mr. Calderon?"

Ray eyed him neutrally for a moment, then shrugged. "I'm an expert. I'm a qualified sharpshooter with both automatic weapons and handguns. But then you knew that already, didn't you?"

"I think I came across the information somewhere," Charlie acknowledged. "Maybe in the paperwork your pal the lieutenant showed me. Along with your dishonorable discharge."

"Look, maybe I wasn't the greatest soldier in the world, but I'm not a psychopath, either. I have absolutely no reason to shoot at anyone and no gun to do it with. And as you just pointed out, if I had wanted to shoot somebody, I probably wouldn't have missed. So what's your beef with me? That I was within a mile or two of whatever happened? Okay, I'm probably guilty of being in the general vicinity. But that's really all I can tell you. So, are you gonna cut me loose, or do I have to get a lawyer?"

Charlie hesitated a moment, then shook his head. "No, sir, you won't have to do that. You're free to go, Mr. Calderon. Deputy Nance will give you a lift back to your car. Thanks for your cooperation."

"If it's all the same, I'll walk back," Calderon said, turning away. "I've enjoyed about as much of Nance's company as I can stand."

"Hey, wait a minute," Owney McClain said, stalking over from the deck. "What the hell's going on here, Charlie? You're not just letting him go, are you?"

"I have no cause to hold him, Mr. McClain. None."

"But damn it, Tim Nance said you had a phone call—"

"An anonymous tip," Charlie nodded, glaring at Nance. "I can't arrest anyone on evidence like that. He could sue the county and end up owning my jail. Let it be, Mr. McClain."

"You let it be, Bauer," Owney said, grabbing Ray's upper arm, spinning him around. "Mister, I don't know what you think you're doing up here, but tourist season's over. You'd better head south with the rest of the sunbirds back to wherever you came from. I'll even buy your ticket and toss in a few bucks for your trouble, but I'm through fooling around with you. You'd better go. Today!"

"Or what?" Calderon said evenly. "Do I disappear, too? Is that how it works?" He yanked his arm free of Owney's grasp, and the two of them would have faced off if Charlie hadn't stepped between them.

"That's enough. Calderon, if you're gonna walk back to your car, you'd best get steppin'. It's a long hike. And Owney, you'd better back off. This man's free to go and that's it. If you lay hands on him again, we'll have to go down to the station and talk about it. Understand?"

"Fine, let him go," Owney said, flushing. "Stay as long as you want, Calderon. You may end up staying for the rest of your life, however long that is. But if you think we're all doormats like Bauer here, you're mistaken. I'll protect my family any way I have to." He turned and stalked angrily over to the company prowl car in the Crow's Nest lot, where his uncle and a handful of shop workers were looking on.

Calderon gave me a "What next?" look, then followed Owney off the beach. He pointedly ignored the crew clustered around the car as he walked past them. No one offered any trouble, or even said a word. But it was coming. It was in their eyes. I could almost smell it in the air.

I could think of only one person who might be able to stop it. I made my way to the corner of the deck where Audrey McClain was sitting huddled beneath her shawl. Ross began wheeling her away, but I cut him off.

"I'm sorry our little jaunt went awry," I said, kneeling beside Audrey. "We can finish it another day, though. Anytime you like."

"Of course," she said, "that would be wonderful, dear." I started to say something about Ray, but she dismissed me with a wave. "I'm sorry," she said, "I have to leave now. I'm very tired." She motioned at Ross and he wheeled her off toward her van.

147

At the corner of the building, he glanced back at me with a faint smile. Of triumph? I couldn't tell. He wasn't easy to read. But Audrey had been. When I'd spoken to her, there was no hint of recognition in her eyes. I don't think she had the vaguest notion of who I was.

29

A WALK IN THE WILDWOOD

∿∿

"HEY, SAILOR, wanna go for a ride?" Ray had walked only a few blocks from the Nest when I caught up to him in my Jeep.

"Yeah, definitely," he said gratefully, climbing in. "I didn't want to spend another second in that damned police car, but I'd forgotten how far away mine actually was. Any chance you can give me a lift to it?"

"No problem. I'd planned to take the afternoon off anyway, and right now a quiet drive in the country sounds like a terrific idea."

"It must have been rough out there. Are you all right?"

"I'm a little shaky," I admitted. "At the time, I was too busy to worry. I um . . . I don't suppose you'd have any idea why someone would shoot at us?"

"Someone other than me, you mean?"

"No, that's not what I meant."

"I don't know why not; everyone else seems to think so. And you really don't know me all that well."

"That's true. And from the little I do know, I'd guess you're capable of doing serious damage to someone if you thought it was necessary. But I can't see where taking potshots at us would do you any good. And I also think you'd make a better job of it.

149

You're a soldier. You know about guns and how effective they are at what ranges. Whoever shot at us should have tried to get closer. I'm just glad he didn't know any better. He came close enough as it was."

"I saw the hole in the boat," Ray said. "Were you at the tiller when the shooting started?"

"That's right. With Audrey beside me."

"So the shooter didn't miss by much. A few feet off the mark at two hundred–plus yards is pretty good shooting. I wonder how good a shot Owen was. Or is."

"He was a soldier once. Plus, he grew up around here. This is hunting country. Almost everyone can shoot."

"Even you?"

"I'm no Annie Oakley, but I know one end of a gun from the other. But the same question applies to Owen as to you. Why would he shoot at us?"

"Maybe to accomplish what nearly happened. To get the locals fired up enough to run me off. It almost worked. If that rent-a-cop hadn't gotten in Bauer's face, he might have put me on a plane himself. Or tried to, anyway."

"Assuming Owen is around—which I'm not—if he wanted to rouse the locals, he could shoot in Audrey's general direction anytime. Why wait until she was with me?"

"Maybe to make sure Sheriff Bauer took it personally. I get the impression you and Bauer are more than just friends. He has a personal interest in you, right? Not that I blame him. But if I've noticed, other people may have, too. Owen, or whoever."

"You're wrong. Charlie and I are friends, and that's it."

He glanced at me, but I kept my eyes on the road. "That's not it," he said. "Not for him, anyway. And I think you know it."

"We must be spending too much time together," I said. "You're starting to sound semirational."

"I hope so. That I sound rational, I mean. But I don't think we're spending too much time together. I don't think we're spending nearly enough. What about you?"

I didn't answer. The truth was, he'd been in my thoughts, uninvited, almost constantly now. His touch, and the kiss in front of the drugstore. The truth was, when Hannah had asked me to buy him off, I turned her down at least in part because I didn't want him to go. And the truth was, when he entered a room now, it brightened for me. And when I'd followed him from the beach a few minutes ago and saw him walking alone along the road, my heart lifted.

The truth was . . . I wanted him in my life, and in my arms. But I'm not a schoolgirl anymore. Sometimes I wonder if I ever was, really. I know my own heart well enough to know that love or even lust can never be casual for me. But this time, they were tangled together in a complicated mix. Love is a hobby for some people, an indoor sport. But for a woman who's been hurt, it's no game. It's like tiptoeing in the dark, barefoot, through a room strewn with broken glass.

Unfortunately, the timing was terrible. My life was only a heartbeat from disaster. I had money problems and problems with my son. I simply had no room for the kind of complications that being with Ray might bring. I just couldn't handle it. And so I didn't tell him how I felt. I let the moment pass—again.

"How far is your car?" I asked.

He fished the plat map out of his shirt and checked it. "Take the next left, then another couple of miles. I parked off the road."

"What are all those x-ed off squares on your chart?"

"Areas I've searched. This is wild country; it's easy to get disoriented, so I'm being as methodical as I can."

"From the looks of that map, you've already covered a fair amount of ground."

"But not enough," he said. "So far, all I've really accomplished is some heavy hiking in the woods. Except . . ."

"Except what?"

"The incident this afternoon, the shooting?"

"What about it?"

"If it really was supposed to push Bauer into running me off, then maybe I'm doing something right."

"Or something wrong. Maybe you should take the hint and back off a little. Let Charlie earn his salary."

"No," Ray said. "I think he's a good man, but he's also a busy one. Finding Jimmy isn't his only priority. He's got lots of other things to worry about."

"And you haven't?"

"Of course I have," he said grimly. "That's the problem. I've always had more important things to worry about than Jimmy. That's why he's . . . wherever he is now. Lost. In every sense of the word. But if I can't find him again, at least this time it won't be because I was too busy or didn't care enough to make the effort."

And a door closed between us. I sensed it as clearly as if I'd heard it slam. He simply withdrew emotionally, raised shields, and stepped into a room where I couldn't follow. And I didn't even try. My father used to do exactly the same thing—vanish emotionally when he didn't want to deal with something, usually something that mattered to me. Sometimes I think that his hidden place was where he really lived. Or maybe all men do it—fort up emotionally when things get intense. Maybe it's a guy thing.

To hell with it. I let him go. I had some private brooding of my own to do. And in spite all that had happened, I had the remains of a perfect afternoon for it. The October sun dappled the Jeep's windshield with a dancing pattern of light and shadows as I motored cautiously along the backwoods trail. The forest floor was a gorgeous tapestry of fallen leaves, ocher and umber and scarlet, and vagrant golden leaves were drifting down as we passed.

I rolled the window down and the perfume of the forest, pine and leaf mulch and sassafras, drifted in. The aroma of autumn. School days. New books, new friends, the tangy sweet scent of burning leaves . . .

But this wasn't a schoolyard. We were in the hills. No one

should be burning leaves in the forest. I goosed the Jeep, picking up five miles an hour or so, all I dared to on the snaking, rutted track.

Ray glanced at me curiously. "Is something wrong?"

"I'm not sure," I said. "Do you smell smoke?"

30

FIRE IN THE HILLS

THE CAR was crouched like a wounded animal beside the trail, burned down to its hubs. The fire had scorched a blackened ring around the hulk and three or four satellite blazes were still smoldering in the ground cover near it. I skidded the Jeep to a halt a few yards up the trail, grabbed the emergency folding shovel I carry under the seat, and piled out.

Ray was already stamping out one of the smaller fires. Fortunately, the area was sandy, and vegetation was mostly gorse and quack grass. If he'd been parked in the pines a little farther on, half the county might have burned.

Twenty frantic minutes of kicking and cursing and shoveling put the worst spots out or under control.

"Your car?" I managed to gasp as I buried a guttering pile of brush.

"Looks like the same model I rented," he grunted, wiping his forehead. "It's hard to be sure, considering the shape it's in."

"You don't seem very concerned."

"It's insured and I didn't lose much personal stuff," he said. "A pair of binoculars and a spare jacket. It might turn out to be a fair trade."

"For what?"

"Maybe the ghost just made his first mistake. For one thing, if there was any doubt someone else could have done the shooting, this ought to erase it. I've got a perfect alibi for this. I was in custody when it happened."

"You think the sniper might have done this?"

"Sure," he said, surprised. "Don't you?"

"I don't know," I said, looking around the area for the first time. I circled the smoldering hulk slowly, examining the ground.

"That looks pretty impressive," Ray said. "Do you actually know what you're doing, or did you OD on Grizzly Adams flicks as a kid?"

"I can read sign," I said mildly, "as long as it's not too complicated. But there's none here, or at least not anymore. We scuffed things up too much."

"Well, somebody was obviously here—the car's proof of that."

"Yes, but that's really all it proves. This doesn't make any sense."

"How do you mean?"

"Let's say whoever did the shooting figured you'd be blamed for it. What would he gain by torching your car?"

"The same thing the shooting was supposed to do. Run me off."

"But you left here in a prowl car under arrest. Why would he burn your car, since doing it might get you out of the same jam he just got you into?"

"I don't know," Ray said, frowning. "Maybe he didn't think that far ahead."

"Now you're reaching. If the sniper is the man you're looking for, he hasn't stayed a step ahead of the law all these years by being stupid."

"Then maybe he didn't handle it personally. He's still got family up here, and all the friends money can buy. Maybe one of the guys working for him isn't a Rhodes scholar. . . ."

He paused, listening. I heard it, too. A car was coming up the trail. I glanced quickly around, but there was no cover sufficient to hide, and it was too late anyway. The car rumbled into view. A county prowl car, thank God. It eased to a halt and Tim Nance stepped out. He leaned on the door a moment, eyeing us through mirrored sunglasses. Then he let the door slam shut and sauntered over, shaking his head.

"Jesus, Calderon, what's your story? You born under a bad sign or somethin'? You're no sooner out of one fix than into another."

"He's not into anything," I said. "Somebody torched his car. It was already burning when we got here."

"Yeah? Well, it was still rented in his name. Maybe trashin' rental cars runs in his family."

"You know I didn't burn it, Nance," Ray said. "I was enjoying your hospitality at the time. What's your problem?"

"That's just it," Nance said, taking a stance a foot from Ray's face, feet wide apart, his thumbs hooked in his gun belt. He was taller than Ray by three or four inches, and probably outweighed him by sixty pounds. Ray didn't back off an inch. "Seems like our department's got all kinds of problems, lately. It also seems like they started just about the time you and your brother blew into town. We got one guy missing, we've got people shooting at people, and we've got a whole lot of local folks in an uproar, afraid of losing their jobs."

"That's a crock and you know it. None of that has anything to do with me. All I want to do is find my brother."

"Maybe so, but meantime you're makin' my job complicated. I get paid to look out for the citizens of this county, Calderon. Was your brother a citizen? Or just another wetback illegal? What about you? Are you a citizen? Maybe you'd better show me your green card."

"You're way out of line, Nance," I said. "What's the matter with you?"

"It's all right," Ray said, waving me off. "Deputy Nance is trying to get a rise out of me. He wants me to swing at him. Or maybe yank that shiny badge off and shove it where the sun don't shine."

"Well? You wanna try it, greaser?"

"Absolutely," Ray said, smiling. "I'm looking forward to it. But not here and not today. You're not worth the trouble, Nance. Or maybe you are. Were you born around here?"

"What?"

"What's the matter, the question too tough? Have you lived here all your life? Or did you show up more recently? Ten years ago? Twenty?"

"What's that to you?"

"Maybe nothing. But it's the kind of question I'm going to keep asking. Tell your boss that, whoever he is."

"I work for Huron County, Calderon. And so does Charlie Bauer, though he may find himself out of a job pretty soon if he doesn't start remembering who pays his salary."

"And whom would that be?"

"The people of this county. The everyday folks who pay the taxes around here."

"I see. And it wouldn't be that some of those good folks get a little more service for their tax dollars, would it? Like Owney McClain, for instance? Or his uncle?"

"I'm here as an officer of the law in the line of duty," Nance said coldly. "But as a private citizen, man to man, I'm suggestin' real strongly that you move on. Go back where you came from. Leave us alone."

"And my brother? Do I just forget about him?"

"If we find him, we'll mail him to ya in a box. How's that sound?"

"Not very likely," Ray said. "I'm beginning to think you clowns couldn't find your butts in a phone booth. So if anyone's going to find my brother, I guess I'll have to do it myself."

"You can try," Nance said grimly. "But I'll lay odds you don't last long. And you, Mitch, you'd better think about what you're gonna do after Speedy Gonzales here gets run off. People in this town got long memories."

"I hope so," Calderon said. "I'm kinda counting on that."

157

31

AN INVITATION TO A DANCE

It took over an hour to report the fire and sign our statements for the elderly retiree who was holding down the desk at the sheriff's department. He was a nice old gentleman, but he really didn't have a clue as to what to do about the car. He tried to raise Charlie on the radio, but he was off scouring the foothills, trying to locate some campers who might have been in the area of the shooting.

It was nearly dusk when we finally pulled into the Crow's Nest parking lot. I switched the engine off, but neither of us got out for a moment. We simply sat in the sudden silence, adrift in our separate thoughts. It had been one helluva day.

I'm not sure which of us realized we hadn't moved or spoken for a while, but we glanced at each other simultaneously. And our eyes met, and we smiled. That was all. Just a shared smile. But in that stillness, something had changed between us, and I think we both knew it. Sometimes a quiet moment can tell you more about someone than all the cocktail chitchat in the world.

"I have to go in," I said at last. "Red's been catching for me all afternoon without a break and things look busy. What about you?"

"I need to shower some of this soot off for openers," he said ruefully, examining the backs of his hands. "Then I guess I'd better try to arrange for another rental car."

"You can take my Jeep if you like. I won't need it for a few hours."

"Thanks, I'd appreciate it. I'll get cleaned up, make some calls, and . . . meet you here later? Eightish or so?"

"Fine, I'll be here," I said, climbing out. "I'd tell you to have a nice day, but I think it's too late. Take care."

"You, too," he said, sliding behind the wheel. He began backing out of the parking slot, then stopped and rolled down the window. "Mitch," he said, scanning the parking lot. "You said the Nest looks busy. Busier than usual?"

"Maybe a little. Why?"

"Just wondered. Maybe I'll call the rental company from here, if you don't mind," he said, turning off the Jeep.

"I don't need an escort," I said as he climbed out. "I've been taking care of myself for a while now. Besides, I own the joint."

"I know that. I just want to use the phone."

The dining room was half-full, mostly mom-and-pop family groups, tourists, I supposed. I didn't know many of them. One of our part-time waitresses was serving in the dining area, and Red was behind the bar, mixing something exotic. Everything seemed normal enough. And yet it wasn't, quite. There was an edgy, uneasy air in the place. The room seemed to have fallen nearly silent when Ray and I stepped in. Or maybe I was just paranoid after the long day. Red briskly poured the concoction she'd been mixing into an iced mug, placed it on a tray, and carried it through the crowd to us.

"Hi, boss," she said brightly. "Nice to see you. Good news—we've been busy as the dickens. Now do me a small favor: Make a quick U-turn, and you and your friend get the hell out of here. Right now."

"Why? What's wrong?"

"Nearly every customer in here works at the fuels plant," she

159

said, still smiling. "Coincidence? I don't think so. Now move it, please."

"She's right," Ray said, "we'd better go."

But it was too late. The door behind us opened and Gordon McClain and Pake Hemmerli stepped in, still wearing their plant security uniforms. Three of the men sitting with their families in the dining area stood up as soon as they saw McClain, and several more began drifting toward us from the bar.

"No need for any trouble now, Mitch," McClain said. "We just want to talk to Mr. Calderon. In private."

"It's all right with me, McClain," Ray said calmly, turning to face him. "Why don't we talk outside?"

"No, it's not all right," I said, stepping between Ray and Gordon McClain. "If you want to talk, you can damned well do it in here. In front of witnesses. Why don't you use one of the tables in the dining room. Among all the wives and kiddies."

"Mitch, you'd best get out of our way," Hemmerli said, grasping my wrist. "You got trouble enough already."

"Ruby!" Red called to the dining room waitress. "Would you call the police, please. We have a problem here."

"Grab her!" Hemmerli yelled. "Don't let—" And I kicked him, hard, in the deep south. And all hell broke loose. Hemmerli stumbled to his knees, gagging, but he still had a death grip on my wrist and he pulled me down with him. McClain jerked a nightstick out of his belt and swung wildly at Ray's head. The blow missed Ray but caught Red solidly across the forearm, spinning her into the flannel-shirted goons charging us from the bar. Ray hammered McClain with a stiff body blow that sent him backward over a table, then whirled to face the pair from the bar. Too late. One of them tackled him from the side and then I lost track of him as the world dissolved into a whirlwind of kicks and curses and wrestling bodies.

I slammed Hemmerli's hand against the edge of a table and pulled myself free just in time to catch somebody's elbow in the temple and go down again. Dazed, I clutched at the knees of one of the rowdies struggling with Ray and managed to drag him down in a desperation tackle. We both fell across Hemmerli, who was still doubled over, retching, clutching his family jewels. He recovered long enough to swing hard at my face, grazing my cheek, which was a big mistake. He was off balance as Red gave him a perfect Rockette kick that caught him dead center in the chest, sending him over backward, out cold.

Gordon McClain stormed back into the fray, swinging his stick, but Red grabbed him from behind as he passed, clamping her right forearm around his throat, pulling him off balance. Still on my knees, I managed to grab the stick, jerked it out of his hands, and rammed it into his midsection. He crumpled, gasping, and Red let him fall. She'd gone deathly pale, wincing as she clutched her left arm. I staggered to my feet and waded into the cluster of men struggling with Ray, swinging McClain's billy like a baseball bat, slamming heads, shoulders, I didn't care. I was lost in the rage of it, bent on doing as much damage as I could—

"HOLD IT!" Charlie Bauer roared in a deafening bellow that seemed to shake the room, freezing everyone. "That's enough, damn it! Now, everybody stay right where you are." He and Tim Nance moved into the mob, separating us, none too gently. He stopped short when he got to me, looking first at the nightstick, then at me with utter consternation.

"Mitch, what the hell's going on here?"

"It was Calderon," Gordon McClain gasped, struggling to his feet. "He was looking for trouble and—"

"Right," Charlie snapped, cutting him off. "He was feeling so froggy, he jumped all six of you, is that it? And Mitch and Red, did they jump you, too, Gordo? Does anybody else want to look me in the eye and tell me that's how it happened?"

No one spoke; maybe we were all too winded.

Charlie took the nightstick out of my hands. "Where'd you get this? From McClain?"

I nodded. It was all I could manage.

"Figures," Charlie said. "And did he use it?"

"He used it all right," Red said quietly. "I think he may have broken my arm with it." She was leaning against a table, holding her left arm tightly against her side with her right. Her color had drained completely now, and her wrist was twisted at an unnatural angle. Ray pushed past one of the shop rats and eased Red down into a chair. He didn't look much better than she did. His jaw was swollen and a cut above his eye was streaming blood down his cheek. He didn't seem aware of it.

"Somebody call an ambulance," Charlie snapped. "Nance, take Mr. McClain here out to the car and read him his rights, assault with intent. Hemmerli, too. As for the rest of you, I'm surprised at the lot of you. You're better men than this and we've got a better town than this. I'm giving you sixty seconds to clear the room. Anybody who's here after that can spend the night in the slammer tonight next to Gordo here. Any takers?"

"You're arresting me?" McClain said, enraged. "What about Calderon? This whole thing's his fault."

"After Mr. Calderon gets medical treatment, he may want to reconsider his vacation plans for the next few weeks. But that'll be between him and me. Now, everyone who doesn't have business here, clear out. Let's go."

They went, the lot of them. But there were no apologies as they pushed past Ray or Charlie or even Red. They were working men, roughnecks. Up here, they're called cedar savages. But never to their faces. Most of them had been swinging axes and chain saws in the piney woods since they were old enough to lift them. When the timber business crashed, they stayed on here and grubbed out a living as best they could. The fuels plant was their salvation, their only chance for a decent life, and anyone threatening it was an enemy—a blood enemy. This scuffle wasn't the end of anything. It was barely the beginning.

32

DAMAGE CONTROL

AT THE emergency room, a harried intern gave me an ice pack for the welt on my cheek and dabbed antiseptic on a cut I didn't even know I had at the corner of my mouth. It took four stitches to close the gash on Ray's forehead and afterward they toted him off to x-ray his bruised ribs.

I slipped into Red's room for a few moments, and she greeted me with a woozy smile. Her tanned, wind-roughened skin was dark against the hospital sheets, but her face was still gray. And seeing her like this, helpless, wounded, made me realize how much I'd come to rely on her strength and spirit over the past year. I'd taken it for granted, and perhaps her, as well. She'd seemed indestructible to me. Or maybe I just needed her to be. But she wasn't. No one is. I leaned over the bed and rested my cheek on hers a moment.

"Hey," she murmured, "that feels great. Why don't we try mouth-to-mouth next? I guarantee you'll never go back to boys."

"If things get much weirder, I may just take you up on that." I sighed, easing into the chair beside her bed. "You look like hell. How do you feel?"

"Never better, honest to God. Mitch, do me a favor. Find out whatever it is they gave me for pain and let's buy the franchise.

I'm over the moon, girlfriend. Feeling this good is almost worth a broken arm. Heck, go ahead and break my other one."

"How is your arm?"

"How should I know? I can't feel it, or much of anything else. Okay, okay, the good doctor said it's a clean break, no problems. They're going to wait for the swelling to go down before they put a cast on it. Probably midmorning tomorrow. How are you doing?"

"I'm fine."

"Funny, you don't look fine," she said, squinting at me. "Your cheek's swollen and you look like a chipmunk with a mouthful of acorns. Are your teeth all right?"

"They're okay; the swelling makes it look worse than it is. No major damage—he barely hit me."

"Hemmerli, wasn't it? I remember kicking him right after. Felt something give. With any luck, I may have broken a few of his ribs. God, it felt great."

"What did? Kicking in his ribs?"

"You bet, girlfriend, though to be honest, right now you could chain me naked to a cactus and whip me with barbed wire and I'd probably enjoy every minute."

"You really are stoned, aren't you?"

"To the bone. You ought to try it sometime."

"I did once. It's how I became a mother."

"You're kidding. No, you're not. You never kid. Okay, you've gotta tell me the story sometime. But wait until I'm a little straighter. Right now, I can barely remember my name. Who are you, anyway?"

"A friend on her way out. Can I get you anything?"

"Nah, I'm okay, really. Fine as wine, in fact. How's your buddy, what-his-name? Ray?"

"He's all right, I guess. He's down getting x-rayed."

"He's got a lotta sand, that guy. Maybe too much. He was going to go outside with those goons until you butted in."

"Don't you think I should have?" I asked.

"I don't know what else you could have done. Besides, a riot in the Nest isn't that big a deal. When your dad ran the place, we had 'em once a week. People used to reserve tables to be sure they'd have a good seat. Semiserious question, Mitch: Are you getting semiserious about Calderon?"

"I don't know," I said honestly. "Maybe. Maybe I am. Why?"

"I thought you might be. You keep your guard up pretty high, but you aren't all that hard to read. At least not for me. But here's the thing, girlfriend. I had a lover once, a few years ago. She was a terrific girl in a lot of ways—witty, bright. Fun to be around, and even better in bed. Maybe the best ever for me. But she was a major problem, too. You see, she swung both ways and she had a redneck hunk boyfriend who was a psycho Jehovah's Witness or something. He worked over my car with a baseball bat one night and tore up my apartment another time. He also roughed up my ladylove more than once. But I could never get her to press charges against him or even get a restraining order. And after a while, it dawned on me that she actually liked it."

"Liked what? Getting beaten up?"

"No, not that, exactly. I think she liked . . . conflict. She needed it. Maybe it gave her an adrenaline high or something, I don't know. I'm no shrink. Anyway, I finally realized that as long as I was with her, my life would always be a shambles. And the bottom line was, as much as I cared about her, I wasn't willing to live like that. Not even for her."

"What are you saying? That you don't want to be my friend anymore? Just because of a crummy broken arm?"

"No." She grinned wanly. "This wasn't your fault. Nobody made me butt in, and I'd do it again in a second. I'm just saying that before you get your heart all tangled up with this guy, you'd better ask yourself if he's really worth the trouble. And if you decide he is, then maybe you'd best reserve a room here. I have a feeling you'll need it. For somebody."

"What happened tonight wasn't Ray's fault."

"I know that. Nothing that's been happening around here is his fault, exactly. And yet here we are."

"Yeah," I said, taking a deep breath, looking around the sterile, anonymous room. "Here we are."

33

INTO THE NIGHT

RAY WAS facing away from me when I stepped out of the elevator. He was sitting on a bench in the hallway outside the emergency room. His back was straight, feet flat on the tiled floor, his hands in his lap. He could have been a robot someone had switched off. Or a statue, *Soldier Waiting*. He looked composed, and patient. And a part of me melted. Because I knew he wasn't. He was near the end of himself. Close to his breaking point, whatever it was. I don't know how I knew, but I did—with absolute certainty. And I also knew what the knowing meant. Yesterday, his heart had been a mystery to me. And now, somehow, I could read him. Like a book, or the opening chapters of one. Red was right. I could be in a lot of trouble.

"Hi," I said quietly, easing down on the bench beside him. "How did your pictures turn out?"

"Not too bad. I've got a couple of cracked ribs and some torn cartilage. They've got my chest taped up like something in *The Mummy's Curse.* Which is about how I feel. How's Red?"

"Stoned. Her arm's broken. They're going to keep her overnight."

"Jesus," he said softly. "I can't tell you how sorry I am about all this."

"It wasn't your fault," I said automatically.

He turned slowly to face me. "Of course it was. Look, when I said I was going to find my brother no matter who got hurt, I thought I had nothing to lose. That the only ones who'd be paying dues would be McClain or his friends or even his family. It never occurred to me that people I . . . care about might get hurt, too. I need to rethink this thing. It's out of control."

"Fine," I said, getting up. "I know a good spot for thinking. Let's go."

"Where?"

"To my place."

"Your place? You mean the Nest?"

"No, my house. I've got a cottage on Ponemah Point."

"No," he said, shaking his head. "The way things are, it's too dangerous for you to be with me. Funny, these past few days I've been racking my brain to figure a way to spend some time alone with you. And now it's here, and I'll have to pass. You've had trouble enough because of me."

"It may be riskier for us to be apart. Those goons from the plant won't give up just because Charlie's got their boss in jail. They'll find you at your motel even if they have to go door to door."

"Then they might find me at your place, too."

"Possibly. On the other hand, suppose they try there first? And there I'll be, all alone, wringing my little hands, trying to convince a surly mob that you're not with me, begging them not to wreck my humble cottage. Is that what you want?"

He arched an eyebrow. "You've never wrung your hands in your life. If you told me you'd wrung someone's neck, now that I might believe. And how did you know where it was?"

"Where what was?"

"My Randolph Scott button," he said, getting up.

"My dear sir," I said primly. "Ah declare, I haven't the foggiest notion of what you're ravin' on about."

"Yeah, right," he said. "Frankly, my dear, you don't give a damn, and I'm too tired to argue. Let's go."

It was a *Wuthering Heights* kind of night, misty, with a hint of drizzle in the air. We didn't talk much on the drive to the cottage. It's a dozen miles from Huron Harbor—on the tip of Ponemah Point, a lone fingerling peninsula that juts into the vastness of Lake Huron from the southeastern shore of Thunder Bay.

The yard was brightly lit by the solar security lamp above the boathouse when we pulled in. I sat a moment, looking the place over. It's old and isolated, a quaint fieldstone and clapboard beachfront box built in the 1880s by a lumber baron who must have been half hermit. The lawn needed mowing, and the house would need paint next summer. If I'm still here, that is.

"Anything wrong?" Ray asked.

"No, I was just . . . feeling the place. I grew up here, and I probably literally know every inch of the point. I don't think anyone's been here. And no wisecracks about women's intuition, okay?"

"Far be it from me," he said, climbing out. "I'm a great believer in intuition. I like this place. It feels friendly."

"Most people think it's lonely."

"It doesn't feel that way to me. But then, I'm not alone here, either. Maybe that's the difference."

I let that pass. He followed me into the house, glancing around. And so did I. It was an odd sensation, seeing my home as though it were new to me, through the eyes of a stranger.

Spartan. There was no other word for it. Two bedrooms, a kitchen, living room, and bath. Lacquered knotty pine walls and hardwood floors. The furniture, what there was of it, was handcrafted of oak, and probably as old as the house. The cushions on the couch and chairs were brown canvas. At least they were new. I'd replaced them when I moved in, but other than that, I'd made no changes to speak of. I'd kept to the motif of the place. North-country funky chic.

"Very nice," he said, wandering to the bay windows in the living room. "Do you have a view of the lake?"

"On a clear night, you can see the north shore across the bay about a dozen miles. To the east, the nearest land is the Canadian shore, a hundred and fifty miles or so. Would you like anything? Coffee or a sandwich?"

He didn't reply. "Ray?"

"What?"

"I asked if you wanted something to eat."

"Sorry, I, ah . . . No thank you."

"My God, you're out on your feet, aren't you?"

"Yeah, I guess I am. It's been a long day, but no longer than yours."

"True, but I don't have broken ribs. My son's room is all made up; the bath's at the end of the hall. Go to bed, for God's sake."

"What are you going to do?"

"I'm going to stay up for a while. I'm too wired to sleep. Look, we'll be all right here. I'm a light sleeper. If anyone shows up, I'll hear them, and I keep my grandfather's thirty-thirty in my bedroom. So go lie down before you fall down."

"Mama always said never to argue with a lady with a rifle. There is one thing, though. You've really gone above and beyond the call of duty to help me. I just want you to know—"

"I know. Good night, Ray. If anything happens, I'll wake you."

"Right." He nodded, raising his hands in surrender. "Good night." He wandered down the hall to Corey's room. I made myself a cup of cinnamon tea, carried it to the living room, and sat in my father's favorite chair, facing the lake. The drizzle had stopped and the fog was thinning a bit. The moon was rising, glowing through the mist, half-hidden behind the pines along the shore.

Looking out at the night, I began to gather my thoughts, to work through the events of the day. Gunfire. I could hear it in my memory almost as clearly as I'd heard it that afternoon. Audrey had been cheerfully rattling on about something, and then, the shots. But Audrey had said something a few minutes before it happened, something about seeing a red car. Possibly Ray's. But she apparently hadn't mentioned it to Owney, or he would have asked Charlie about it. Perhaps she forgot. Ross said she had good and bad days, and she had definitely gone foggy by the end of the afternoon.

Okay, she forgot about it. But I hadn't. And I hadn't told Charlie about it, either, before or after the fire. The burned-out hulk was well back in the woods. It wouldn't have been visible from the lake. So either Audrey was mistaken about seeing a car—unlikely, since not much in the forest looks like a red car—or there were two red cars up there. Possible. Or Ray had lied about where he'd been when the shots were fired.

I didn't like this last possibility much. I could rationalize the lie, if that's what it was. He was in a jam and didn't trust Charlie. He might have lied to cover himself, and I could understand that. But if that was so, he had also lied to me about it. And I couldn't understand that. Or maybe I just didn't want to.

God, my head felt like gerbils were jogging in it. I finished the last of my tea, rinsed the cup, then toddled down the hall to my room. Ray's door was open and I looked in on him as I passed. He'd taken off his shirt and shoes and collapsed under his jacket on Corey's bed. Asleep, his face seemed younger and surprisingly gentle, almost boyish. It was his eyes that made him seem older, more intense. Either way, awake or asleep, I found him absolutely magnetic. I wanted to touch his cheek, to cover him with a blanket or something. But he'd been so groggy earlier . . .

Instead, I went to my own room. The antique oak lodge bed looked wonderfully inviting, but first I got my grandfather's .30-30 Winchester out of its locked case in the closet, loaded it, and parked it between the nightstand and my bed. Only then did I allow myself the luxury of lying down for moment, to rest and to think.

171

And to crash. I was dead to the world approximately one and a half seconds after my head touched the pillow, so completely asleep that when something snapped me awake in the night, it took me a moment to remember where I was.

34
STRANGERS IN THE DARK

I LAY there for a moment, listening, collecting myself, trying to remember the sound that had roused me. Nothing. I'd been dreaming—I had a vague memory of being on the boat with Audrey—but it was gone now, and my heart was pounding and my breathing was shallow as I listened intently for whatever night sound had awakened me. It must have been a noise of some sort, but I could hear nothing but my own hammering heart. The clock radio on the nightstand read 3:10. The phone was silent, and Ray had been so exhausted, I doubted he was up moving around. . . .

A floorboard creaked in the living room. Someone was definitely out there. I eased off the bed and picked up the rifle. Some people are afraid of guns, and rightly so. A gun can do terrible damage quicker than any tool on earth. They're never truly safe, even when they're supposedly empty. But the familiar feel of the worn stock of my grandfather's old weapon felt greatly reassuring to me. If someone had broken into my home, they were in more trouble than I was.

I moved quietly down the hall, barefoot, still wearing the clothes I'd had on earlier. I glanced into Corey's room as I passed, but it was too dark to see anything. I flattened myself against the wall at the end of the hall, listening, holding the rifle waist-high and ready. I sensed someone moving in the living room, and I stepped out to face them.

Ray was standing at the bay window, arms folded, looking out at the night. He glanced at me and our eyes met. "Sorry, I didn't mean to wake you. I tried to be as quiet as I could." His voice was barely a whisper, though there was no one left to waken. Moonlight and shadows were shifting slowly through the room as though we'd been lifted to the clouds.

"Is anything wrong?" I asked.

"No, I just couldn't sleep. The bandages on my ribs make it difficult to breathe lying down."

I knew the feeling. I was having trouble with my breathing, too. His eyes were still on mine and I couldn't look away.

"I want to hold you," he said at last, his voice still a husky whisper. "I need you close to me. Would that be all right?"

I nodded. It was all I could manage. He didn't move toward me, so I moved to him, joining him in the moonlight. I leaned the rifle against the couch and we . . . melted together, an embrace so fluid, it felt like liquid light pouring over me, each part of my body blending with a part of his. God, we were a perfect match. It felt as if we'd done this a thousand times before. Or maybe I'd been waiting for it for a very long time. We didn't kiss; we just stood there, holding each other, warming each other. My lips were against the hollow of his throat. He smelled of wood smoke from the forest, and a muskier, headier scent, a man scent, his alone. I could have stood there a thousand years.

"I think I've wanted to hold you like this since that first night." His voice was so close to my ear, it felt as if I were hearing it from within my own heart.

"Please," I said, instinctively trying to maintain some distance, some composure. "Don't tell me it was love at first sight."

"Absolutely not. You were camouflaged by a ton of diving gear when I first saw you, remember? But later, at the McClain place? I was supposed to be on serious business, but I kept getting distracted. I could already feel the heat."

"You concealed it well enough. Except for one kiss, I wasn't sure you cared for me at all."

"Let's face it, the timing couldn't be worse," he said simply. "It's still awful. I came here to find Jimmy, and I haven't been able to. And meanwhile, I'm falling hard for you, and all I've done is bring you a world of trouble. Everything about this is wrong."

"Everything?"

"Well, okay, not this part. Us together—this feels right. Completely right."

I had no words. I nestled deeper into his shoulder, feeling his pulse warm against my cheek.

He took a deep breath. "Mitch, I feel . . . lost. Maybe I got kicked in the head today or something, but I can't seem to make sense of anything. It's all upside down. I don't know what to do about you, or my brother, about any of it."

"You went through the meat grinder," I said. "We both did. And it's after three in the morning. I think the logical move is to go back to bed. Things will make more sense in the morning."

"Yeah." He nodded, his cheek against mine. "You're right. Go back to bed, please. I'll just sit up out here and think awhile. I doubt I can sleep all taped up like this, anyway."

I looked up at him, and his face, his most interesting face, was in shadow. But I knew exactly where to find his mouth, and I did. "I said we should go back to bed," I said after a moment. "I didn't say anything about going to sleep. Unless of course, you're so banged up you'd . . . rather not."

"I'm a little battered, but I'll do my best. Be gentle with me."

"I think that's my line," I said.

"Not tonight," he said. "Not tonight."

35
MORNING LIGHT

It was a night of smoke. The scent of it was in his hair, and mine, and on our bodies together. Smoke, and with it a smoldering body heat that gradually rose to a flame. We really were gentle with each other, and not only because of the bandages on his chest. It was as though we'd made love many times before and knew we would be together like this many times again. Perfection wasn't necessary. We didn't have to plumb every mystery, discover every hidden pleasure. There would be time for it, time and again. And because we weren't seeking perfection, we very nearly found it. I fell asleep tangled in his arms, wrapped in his legs. And I dreamed of smoke.

And woke to the scent of it. Slowly, deliciously, I floated up through the haze into a drowsy awareness, keeping my eyes closed, savoring the spell. The autumn glow of morning light was warm on my eyelids, suffusing me, and I wanted the moment to linger. I lay there, wreathed in memories. And I licked my lips, savoring the taste of . . . smoke.

And I realized it wasn't just a memory. I really did smell smoke, or something like it. I opened my eyes. I was alone, in the tangle of my bedclothes. Ray was gone. And it wasn't smoke in the air; it was the incredible perfume of bacon frying. It was nearly nine. The room was a shambles, sheets dangling from the bed, clothing lying where it had fallen. And it looked positively golden, as fine as any Park Avenue penthouse suite.

I could hear the radio murmuring in the kitchen, Huron Harbor news, farm reports or something. And I swear I could even hear the sizzle of bacon. I found my frayed terry-cloth robe in the closet, and for a moment, I wished I had something nicer. But only for a moment. In my heart, I knew it wouldn't matter. We were beyond all that now.

Ray was in the kitchen, barefoot, wearing a faded forest green flannel shirt and Levi's a size too large for him. His hair was tousled, still damp from the shower. I sensed some wariness in him. And I understood it. We weren't children. We'd both been through morning-afters. They can be terribly complicated. And sometimes grim.

"And he cooks, too," I said. "Is there no end to this young man's talents?"

"I hate to bust your bubble, but I'm afraid my cooking's limited to guy stuff, bacon and eggs, scorched burgers, chow that bypasses the tum and heads directly to your arteries."

"It smells wonderful. And I think you may already have put my heart at risk."

He glanced up at me quizzically but let it pass. "I found these clothes in the bedroom closet. Mine are pretty grubby, so I borrowed them. I hope . . . no one minds."

So that was it, or part of it. "No," I said casually, leaning against the doorway, folding my arms, "I'm sure he won't mind."

"Who won't?" he said, exasperated.

"My dad," I said. "They're his. I keep them around to . . . Well, I've just kept them, that's all."

"I see," he said, visibly relaxing. "Sorry, they're a little big on me. I thought they might be Charlie Bauer's size."

"And if they were?"

"I don't know," he said simply. "We're on new ground here, Mitch. I don't have a map."

"I haven't either. But we've found our way this far without

177

one. And I don't feel a bit lost. Quite the opposite, in fact. I feel . . . found. How about you?"

He hesitated a moment before he answered. And in that split second, every defensive shield I've built over years as a surviving single snapped into full alert. I didn't even hear his answer—something about feeling the same way. It was the right thing to say, but somehow that silent instant was more telling.

"Do I have time enough for a quick shower before your handiwork hits the table? I feel like wreckage."

"You've got four minutes exactly, but it's not necessary, you know," he said, meeting my eyes. "You look fine to me just the way you are. Just fine." Again, the right thing to say. But a moment too late.

I padded down the hall, toward the bath. And the morning sun wasn't as golden, and the bedroom just looked a mess as I passed. I stopped, eyeing it a moment, remembering. And then I turned and retraced my steps.

Ray glanced up, surprised. "What's wrong?" I said. "And please don't jerk me around. I know something's up."

"I've . . . got to leave," he said simply. "I've got to go back to Virginia."

"Why?"

"Unfinished business. I told you I've been doing undercover work, infiltrating the crowd Jimmy was running with. Well, I haven't been working alone. Other people are involved, people I vouched for. By pulling out, especially after Jimmy's disappearance, I'm putting them at risk. Nobody's more paranoid than dopers. Nobody. They won't believe Jimmy's disappeared and that I'm off looking for him. They'll come up with their own spacey explanations. And people might just get killed—people who were counting on me to cover for them. I have to go back."

"You knew all this when you told Galloway to take a hike. What changed your mind?"

"You did."

"I did? How?"

"After you . . . passed out on me last night, I held you for what was left of the night. Thinking. Want to know what I came up with?"

"I'm listening."

"Jimmy's dead. I've known it from the first. And the man who killed him is still here. Everything that's happened points to it."

"There might be other explanations," I said.

"Do you really believe that?"

"You're talking. I'm still listening."

"All right. He's here, but he's had years to camouflage himself, to build a solid cover. I've been blundering around like a bull at a bake sale, hoping to flush him out. But I underestimated him. Or perhaps them, depending on who's involved. I'm still going to find him, but it may take some time. A year, maybe five, for all I know. I just don't know. But meanwhile, the situation has gotten out of control here. The way things are, maybe the best thing for me to do is back off for a while, let everything cool down before anybody else gets banged up, or worse. My business in Norfolk shouldn't take more than a few weeks. And then I'll be back. Maybe I'll even come back to stay. How would you feel about that?"

"You're asking me what I think now? After you've already decided? What difference does it make what I think?"

"Damn it, Mitch, don't get defensive on me now. Please. It's too important. Last night was too important."

"I thought it was. Now I'm not so sure. Look, you've had all night to work this out," I said. "It's all new to me. I'll need a few minutes to think about it. A shower's worth, say. Save me some bacon."

I kept the water cool, trying to soothe the hurt and keep my anger in check. It wasn't fair. Damn it, it just wasn't! I hadn't been mooning around waiting for Mr. Right or even Mr. Right for Tonight. I had a hectic life of my own, complete with my fair share of problems. When I'd first sensed myself being drawn to Ray, I'd fought it. Well, sort of. At least I hadn't thrown myself at him. I thought my feelings were too hot not to cool off a little and I fully expected things to derail. But they hadn't. And then last night happened. And it was . . . the finest new thing in my life in a very long time. Maybe the best ever. And, surprise, surprise, it was turning out to be complicated.

Well, why not? We'd both come into this . . . situation carrying luggage. We had histories, problems in our lives. They hadn't gone anywhere, hadn't just magically disappeared in the dark. So . . . if last night really meant anything, if it was as important as it felt to me, then somehow we would work this out. Hell, nothing good in my life ever happened conveniently, not my son, not my work, none of it. Why should falling in love be different? If that's what we were doing.

Aye, there's the rub. Suppose we weren't? Suppose all last night ever amounted to was . . . last night? Well, then I'd deal with it. But in my heart, I was sure it wouldn't work out that way. And I'd do almost anything to keep it from happening.

I toweled myself dry, gave my hair a lick and a promise (the wet look is in, somewhere, I think), threw on jeans and a sweatshirt, and padded back to the kitchen, ready for the world.

Ray had set the table, breakfast looked scrumptious, and he was holding the telephone receiver. "It's for you."

I took it. And I even recognized the voice. She rattled on nonstop. I couldn't have gotten a word in edgewise if I'd wanted to. But I was so stunned, I couldn't think of much to say anyway. Except, yes, yes, that I'd be in later that afternoon, and to thank her for calling.

When I hung up, Ray was pouring coffee, fresh and black. And trying hard not to seem curious. "That was Mrs. Maybry, the loan officer from the bank. My paperwork's been approved. They're giving me a line of credit."

"That's terrific. But I thought there was some kind of a problem about that."

"There was," I said, taking a deep breath. "But now it seems I have a cosigner for my note. Audrey McClain."

"Oh," Ray said, filling my cup but avoiding my eyes. "Well, that's . . . good news."

36

A DEGREE OF SEPARATION

❧

"IT COMES down to a matter of trust," I said. We were in my Jeep, headed into Huron Harbor.

"No, it doesn't," Ray said. "I do trust you, and I trust your judgment. But when you accept a favor from someone, especially a serious favor, you can't help feeling obligated. By your sense of honor, if nothing else."

"I might feel obligated if this was actually costing Audrey anything," I agreed. "But it's not. She's offered to cosign a note for me that'll save my financial neck, but she won't have to put up a dime. As long as I make the payments—and I'm sure I can—there'll be no problem at all. Ray, this means a lot more than just saving my business to me. It's my chance for a place and a life of my own, and a home for Corey and me to be together."

"I understand that."

"I'm not sure you do. But let's say you're right, that Audrey really is trying to buy me off somehow. How would it work? At some point she says either I slip you a dose of arsenic or else? Do you think I'd spike your coffee or whatever just because she's signed her name on a few papers?"

"It might not be that simple."

"It would be for me. If she thinks she's buying any part of me, she's mistaken. And so are you."

"Maybe you're right."

"Maybe?" I echoed, feeling an angry red sunrise seething just below my mental horizon. "Or maybe not? Maybe I might sell out a friend for a few bucks, assuming we really *are* friends. Well, here's something with no maybes to it, *Mr.* Calderon. If I don't accept Audrey's offer, I'm going to lose everything I've built here, along with my last chance to share my son's childhood while he's still in it. And if avoiding that involves a risk, then it's one I have to take."

"Fair enough."

"What does that mean?"

"It means all right, I understand. Whatever comes up, we'll work it out."

"Good," I said, still feeling angry and more than a little defensive. "When's your flight?"

"Seven tonight. Can you drop me at the rental agency? I'll need a car for the day."

"You're going to keep searching?" I said. "After what happened yesterday?"

"*Especially* after what happened yesterday. Besides, there was an area farther back that looked interesting. I might need your help to check it out, though. Think you might be willing to give me a hand when I get back?"

"*If* you come back, I'll lend you a hand, or anything else you need. And I'll start by loaning you the Jeep," I said, wheeling into the Crow's Nest lot. "There's no need for you to rent a car just for today, assuming they'll rent one to you. I expect I'll be here all day lining up a contractor and whatever. If I need to do any running around, I can borrow Red's pickup. Drop it off when you're done, and I'll give you a lift to the airport. The tank's full, and if you lose the keys, I keep an extra set wired to the front bumper strut. But damn it, try to keep this one from going up in flames, okay? It's the best car I've owned in years."

I pulled up in front of the building and climbed out before he could kiss me. Or I could kiss him.

"I'll see you tonight," he called after me.

"I'll be here," I said, stalking into the Nest. I headed straight for my office, still upset with Ray, and with me. But most of all, angry because the night was over. And it was morning.

37

REBUILDING THE NEST

ഛ~∾

FORTUNATELY, I had no time to brood. I called Ellen Maybry back and made an appointment to finalize the paperwork, but she assured me it was just a formality. We had a done deal.

So I promptly began making plans to spend the money. I called Red at the hospital and got a few names, and then I started calling contractors to come in and bid for the job. Fall is a slow season for builders. The first contractor showed up at two o'clock, a friend of Red's named Krupka. He looked like a farm boy, towheaded, with a beefy complexion. He seemed far too young to be serious, but he scrambled up into the rafters like Tarzan, took thorough notes, and said he'd crunch the numbers and call me with an estimate by five.

I got the second contractor, a Mr. Overholt, out of the Yellow Pages. He ambled in about three. He was an hour late and roughly a hundred pounds overweight, and he was wearing immaculate Carhart overalls that didn't look as if they'd ever seen a day's work. I offered him the use of the ladder, but he said it wouldn't be necessary, that he'd seen hundreds of these "rot jobs" before. Rot jobs? He spent ten minutes sauntering around the dining area with his hands in his pockets, frowning knowledgeably up at my roof. And then he announced that the whole thing needed to be replaced—the roof, the knotty pine ceiling, and all of the support struts, as well. The struts are oak, nearly a foot thick, and would probably support a freeway overpass. I was trying to ease him out the door politely when a police car screeched to a halt in the parking lot out front.

I read it in Charlie Bauer's face the moment he stepped into the Nest. Trouble. Serious trouble. I cut Mr. Overalls off in mid-spiel, told him I'd call him, maybe, and met Charlie halfway.

"What's happened?" I said.

"Calderon," he said simply. "He's been shot."

I felt as though someone had turned the volume down on the room. "Is he alive?" I asked. And suddenly my eyes were stinging.

"Yeah," Charlie said, glancing away, "but I won't kid you, Mitch, he's in rough shape. Real rough. He may not make it."

"Miss Mitchell," Overholt said, "we really need to talk—"

"Not now," I said. "I said I'd call you."

"Look, little lady, you asked me to come down here, and it's only fair to—"

"You want an answer now? Fine," I snapped, turning on him. "The answer's no. No deal. Good-bye, Mr. Overholt."

"Now wait a minute—"

"Get out!" I roared, and left him stammering as I ran to my office to grab my jacket.

"Mitch, there's no rush," Charlie said, following me inside and closing the door. "Ray's still in surgery at County General and he'll be in intensive care after that. We won't be able to see him for a while. But maybe you can help me. Do you know where he was today?"

"No, I—in the hills, I think. Why?"

"We're trying to trace his movements. He cracked your Jeep up just outside the city limits, on River Road. Sideswiped a parked car and spun broadside. A local trucker stopped to help. He decided not to wait for the ambulance, just drove him straight to the hospital in your Jeep. He said Ray was weaving before the crash but that no other cars were near him, so apparently he was

185

shot somewhere else and he was trying to make it to town."

"How seriously is he hurt?"

"As bad as it gets. He was shot in the head, probably with a small-caliber handgun at close range. The wound showed powder burns. His skull's fractured, his left eye is . . . gone, and the other one's severely injured. So even if he survives the surgery . . ."

I sat down on the edge of my desk. Had to, or I would have fallen. "He'll be blind?" I said, my voice barely a whisper. And for a moment I was in the river again, groping around in the rental car. Lost in black water. Forever.

"Maybe not," Charlie said carefully. "But . . . yeah, he might be. If he makes it at all." He opened my liquor cabinet, poured a stiff brandy into a snifter, and held it out to me. "Here, you look like you need this."

"No," I said. "I'll . . . I'll be all right in a minute."

Charlie hesitated, then knocked back half the brandy with a single swallow, baring his teeth against the bite of it. And somehow, seeing that snapped me out of the fog.

"You don't drink," I said. "I've never even seen you sip a beer."

"That's because you usually see me on duty."

"You're on duty now."

"That's right," he said. He drank down the rest of the brandy, coughed, then stared longingly at the empty glass as though he was considering a refill. "God, Mitch, what the hell's happening? We've got a quiet little town here, and all of a sudden I've got one man missing, probably dead, cars burning, and two shootings in as many days. Jesus, it was awful, blood all over. . . ." His voice was trembling. He carefully placed his glass on the sideboard. "I'm sorry. I didn't mean to rattle on. I've seen bodies before. Maybe I've seen one too many. Your Jeep's still at the hospital. I want to leave it there until an evidence team can get here from Lansing to go over it. Is that okay with you?"

I nodded.

"You said Ray was up in the hills. Any idea where?"

"No. Probably somewhere beyond where his car was burned yesterday. He was being pretty methodical about the search. You know what the hell of it is, Charlie? Today was his last day. He was pulling out. Flying back to Norfolk tonight."

"He was giving up?"

"For the time being," I said. "He wanted to let things cool off here."

"Amen to that. Too bad he didn't go last night. How much ground do you think he could have covered past his car?"

"I don't know. He had a map he was marking off; maybe you can tell from that."

"Possibly, if it turns up. It doesn't seem likely he was shot in the hills anyway. I don't see how he could have driven himself out on those roads in the shape he was in. But if he wasn't up there, then where was he? And what the hell happened?"

"He can tell us when he comes around," I said. "Look, I um . . . I want to go the hospital. Can you give me a lift?"

"There won't be anything you can do, Mitch."

"I know. I want to go there anyway."

"Yeah, I figured you might. Better tell your cook you're done for the day, Mitch. We're liable to be gone awhile."

38
THE WAITING ROOM

༄ৡৢঌ

THE BUSTLE of County General was a blur to me, a waking dream. A harried intern in a blood-spattered green smock told us Ray was alive but still in surgery and still in critical condition. They were trying to contact a specialist from the University of Michigan to do the surgery on his right eye. If Ray survived the night.

Charlie and I sat quietly on plastic chairs in the hall outside the operating room. I don't know how long we waited. A couple of hours, I suppose. At some point, I began to shiver uncontrollably and Charlie draped his jacket over my shoulders.

I raised my head and met his eyes, and tried to read his freckled, familiar face. I've known him half my life, if I've known him at all. "Charlie, can I ask you something? Off the record, just between us? You told Calderon you'd take a serious stab at turning up Owen McClain. Have you done that?"

"I haven't found him, if that's what you mean. I didn't really expect to, but I've still got a few leads to check out."

"So you really have been working on it?"

"Of course. I said I would, and I did. Why?"

"Because, until now, I don't think I took Ray seriously," I said, massaging my eyelids with my fingertips. They felt like they'd been sandpapered. "I mean, I knew he believed it, so I didn't discount it entirely, but down deep, I thought he was wrong. And so did you."

"True enough," he admitted. "Well, I was mistaken and Ray's paid the price for it. I thought keeping Gordon locked up would cool things off, but I was wrong about that, too."

"What about Ross? One of the sketches Megan made looked a little like him. Have you checked him out?"

"He was the first one I checked out, simply because I didn't know much about him. Ross isn't Owen McClain, Mitch."

"You're positive?"

"Absolutely. I can't give you a minute-by-minute history of the guy's life, but I can tell you he's spent a fair chunk of it in various jails. I've got mug shots, fingerprints, the works on him. It's not the kind of identification you could fake even if you wanted to."

"Not even if you had money? A lot of money?"

"My God," Charlie said softly. "You don't believe me, do you? Look, I swear to you, Mitch, on my honor, I can account for most of Ross's life. He's not Owen McClain."

It was in his eyes. Charlie wasn't a simple man, though he worked at giving that impression. I knew I didn't understand his motives, necessarily, nor could I read his thoughts. But I did know he was telling me the truth. Or . . . at least, he thought he was. "You said Ross was in prison?"

"A couple of times."

"For what?"

"Small-time stuff. Bad checks, fraud, con games. Why?"

"I don't know. How does a small-time crook end up with a fat city job like working for the McClains?"

"Gordon got him the job, I believe. He and Ross did time together in the Thumb."

"A con man who just happens to look a little like Owen McClain? That's kind of an odd coincidence, isn't it?"

"I suppose it is," Charlie said thoughtfully. "What are you getting at?"

"I'm just trying to make sense of this, Charlie. And I'm beginning to wonder if we've been looking at it backward the whole time. You keep saying Owen's dead. All right, suppose he is? If he's pushing up daisies somewhere, then why all the trouble? Ray's no threat to a dead man, but he was obviously a threat to something or someone. If you take Owen out of the picture, what's left?"

"I don't know. What do you think is left?"

"The money," I said simply. "All that McClain money. Maybe Owney was afraid that Jimmy was entitled to some of it. Or Gordon was."

"Why should Gordon worry? The way I understand it, he's been pruned from the family tree, more or less."

"Maybe that's it. It must have been tough for Gordon, sitting in jail, thinking about all that money. Suppose he did more than think about it? Suppose he came up with a scam to get his hands on some of it? By bringing in a ringer."

"You mean Ross? Pretending to be Owen? It would never work. For openers, I could prove he was a phony."

"But only if he claimed it openly. Think about it. Owen's still technically a wanted man, so they have the perfect excuse for keeping Ross's identity secret. The only person they'd actually have to convince would be Owney. He controls the money and I think he might be willing to share it with his dear old dad, don't you?"

"Yeah," Charlie said. "Maybe he would."

"Ross has had cosmetic surgery," I said. "I noticed the scars the first time I met him. I assumed he was trying to look younger, but suppose it wasn't? The hell of it is, he wouldn't even have to look much like Owen. Owney's never seen his father, and they'd tell him Ross's surgery was to conceal his identity."

"God knows, Owney's no rocket scientist," Charlie conceded. "He's probably dense enough to go for it. And he's not the only one. I noticed Ross's resemblance to Megan's drawing right off, but after I checked him out, I forgot about him. It didn't occur to me that the resemblance could have been deliberate. If Gordon and Ross are running a con, it would explain a few things—more than a few, in fact. The fight, the shootings, even the fire. Gordon's always been the McClain family black sheep. The old man cut him off years ago and Audrey had no use for him, either. But lately, Owney's been treating him like royalty. Made him head of security at the plant and even gave his old jailhouse buddy Ross a fat job—" His beeper went off.

"Excuse me, Mitch. I have to call in." He hurried off to the nurses' station to use the phone. I'm not sure how long he was gone. My sense of time seemed to be out of focus. Then he was back, kneeling beside me.

"I've got a three-car pileup on South Twenty-three, Mitch. I have to go. Are you going to wait?"

I nodded.

"Okay, if you get a chance to talk to Ray, ask him who shot him. Nothing else, understand? Don't press him. And um, this idea about Ross and Gordon? Let's keep it between us, okay? For now, anyway. I'll check back with you later."

I nodded again, and Charlie trotted off, grateful to be moving, I think. A half hour later, a nurse in surgical greens came out, holding a plastic packet at arm's length in front of her.

"Dr. Kienzle said there's no point in your waiting any longer, miss. They're going to insert a cranial shunt to try to control the cerebral edema. The patient won't regain consciousness for at least six hours, maybe more. These are his clothes. Do you have gloves?"

"Gloves?"

"The pants are soaked," she said briskly, placing the package on the seat beside me. "He soiled himself when he was shot. You should probably wear gloves if you're going to examine them. Sorry, but I have to get back. The doctor said he'd call the station and brief you when we've finished."

"Miss?" I said. But the door to the surgery was already closing behind her. She didn't hear me.

I sat there a moment, numbly eyeing the package of sodden clothing. And I realized she'd left it with me because I was wearing Charlie's jacket. But it was appropriate that she did. Ray had been wearing them, but the shirt and faded Levi's in the bag were my father's.

It was nearly nine in the evening when they wheeled Ray past on his way to post-op. I stood up, but there was nothing to see. His face was a mask of bandages and plaster, and his body was shrouded by a sheet. It could have been anyone, really. Anyone at all. And then I caught his eye, or thought I did. Maybe it was a trick of the light, but he seemed to be staring at me. A flat, feral stare, without recognition or intelligence. They wheeled him into an elevator, and then he was gone. I sank slowly down on my bench, shaken to my soul.

I should have left then, but I didn't. Somehow I felt that leaving would be a betrayal. I don't know why. So I sat.

An hour or so later I came out of my reverie and realized Red was looking down at me. I don't know how long she'd been standing there. She was in street clothes, a sweatshirt and faded jeans. Her left arm was in a plastic cast supported by a sling.

"Hi," she said, easing down on the bench beside me, draping her good arm over my shoulder. We sat there a moment, heads together, not talking, just . . . together. "I've been calling you all day. I finally called Charlie and he told me what happened. How are you doing?"

"I'm okay," I said. "How about you?"

"A few bruises, a headache, and a shiny new cast. I'll live. Charlie asked me to see you get home, Mitch. There's nothing more you can do here tonight. He promised to call you if anything changes."

"I don't know," I said.

"Well, I do," Red said. "Look, you're exhausted. If you hang around here all night, you'll be wasted tomorrow when Ray may really need you. Come on, let's get out of this place. It's making me stir-crazy."

"Yeah," I said. "I know the feeling."

39

ALONE IN THE AFTERMATH

I DROPPED Red at her apartment, then borrowed her pickup to drive myself home to Ponemah Point. She asked me to stay the night with her, but I passed, saying I had to be at my place in case the hospital called. Which was partly true. I also needed some time and space alone to sort things out.

But even at the cottage, I wasn't alone. Ray and I had shared only one night here, yet his presence seemed to hover in the place, haunting it, and me. When I made a cup of cocoa, a memory of bacon scented the air. And when I carried my cup into the living room, I could still see him standing at the window, looking out at the lake.

"On a clear day, you can see halfway to Canada," I'd said, or something like that. And I wondered how far he could see now, or if I'd ever see him again, alive. I sat on the sofa awhile, trying to make sense of what had happened, but nothing would come. I simply couldn't focus. Images kept circling: the hospital hallway, Ray frowning as he poured my coffee after Mrs. Maybry's call, Charlie telling me about the accident, his eyes misty. . . .

Damn it. None of it made sense. But Red was right, if I didn't rest, I'd be of no help to anyone tomorrow.

I washed my face, then lay down fully clothed on my bed. Fell down, actually. I didn't think I could sleep. I was wrong. The faint scent of smoke wafted up from the pillowcase and carried me into a dream of the night before. And I was in Ray's arms, and he was in mine . . . and then he was leaving me, driving away in my Jeep. And then, suddenly, the Jeep stopped. I called out to Ray, but he didn't get out. And the Jeep didn't move. It just sat there, freezing my dream like a film jammed in a projector.

I snapped awake with a start, my heart racing. The bedside clock read 2:20. What had awakened me? The dream? Why? Because of the Jeep. Ray had driven off . . . and then stopped. But that wasn't how it happened. He hadn't stopped. He'd simply driven away. So why had he stopped in my dream? It didn't make any sense . . . unless someone else had stopped.

I rose quietly from the bed, then padded to the kitchen in the dark and peered out into the yard.

Red's pickup was there, sitting silently in the driveway. There was no one else. A dream, that's all it was. And yet it meant something. I knew it intuitively, though I was too groggy to figure it out. Maybe in the morning . . .

40
THE DAWN

I WAS up before the first blush of dawn, on the phone to the hospital. Ray was still alive, but still in critical condition. He hadn't regained consciousness. They wouldn't tell me anything more. Perhaps there was no more to tell.

I was too wired to even consider going back to sleep, so I tried to force myself to sit at the kitchen table, and think things through. Easier said than done. The events of the day and night before kept going around in my head. And soon I found myself imitating them, pacing a slow circular path between the kitchen and the living room, carrying a cup of coffee that had long since gone cold.

Nothing made any sense to me. And if Ray died . . . maybe nothing would again. And if he lived? In some ways that posed even more questions. I kept seeing his eye through the ugly hole in his bandages, the flat, robotic stare. How much of the man who held me, who'd loved me in the night, remained behind that ugly gauze mask? I tried to tell myself it wouldn't matter, that I'd still care for him anyway, blind or maimed or whole. But in my secret heart I knew it was a lie. It would matter. How could it not? I just didn't know how much.

Glancing idly out the window at Red's pickup, I recalled my

groggy dream of the night before. Ray had driven off in the Jeep and then stopped. And in daylight, the answer was transparent. Ray shouldn't have stopped. Not in my dream, nor in those woods the day before. He was too smart to let a stranger get close to him after all that had happened. And yet someone must have, because Charlie had said he'd been shot at close range while he was behind the wheel of the Jeep. But how? And by whom?

Red once said that Ray had too much sand for his own good. So maybe he had stopped to confront someone or . . . that was the problem. There were so many maybes, a mind-boggling army of them. But only one certainty. Someone had gotten close to Ray. And that someone shot him in the face. And even if he lived, he would never be the same. Nor would I. Nor would I.

At some point I passed the plastic bag that contained Ray's clothing. I'd forgotten I had it. Perhaps I should have given the clothes to Charlie; I suppose they were evidence of some sort. But they weren't only Ray's clothes, they were my father's, the last things of his I still had. And the bloodstains were already more brown than red. I carried the bag to the sink. Maybe if I soaked the clothing in cold water, the stain wouldn't set.

Phew! The stench hit me as soon as I opened the bag. I'd forgotten what the nurse said about Ray soiling himself when he was shot. I grimaced, then quickly went through his pockets. The pants were sodden, but at least his pockets were dry. I retrieved his wallet, a pocketknife, and some loose change. The plat of the hill area was in his shirt pocket. More than half of the search grids he'd drawn on it were neatly x-ed out. Maybe Charlie could use it to get some idea of where he'd been when he was shot.

I carried the jeans to the washing machine, lifted the lid to drop them in, then hesitated. Something was wrong about them. The pants pockets—they were completely dry. But if he'd soiled himself . . . I picked up the jeans by the waistband and held them out. They were damp all right, but it couldn't be urine. There was a neat waterline roughly halfway up the thighs. The waist area was bloodstained, but otherwise it was dry.

I raised the pants higher and sniffed the wet area. The stench was definitely funky, but it wasn't urine. Similar, though, and familiar. The rotten-egg odor the nurse had smelled was hydrogen sulfide, a mild chemical stew that sometimes seeps into groundwater near abandoned mines or quarries. It stinks, but it's harmless. I've even dived in it a few times, exploring old mine shafts in the Upper Peninsula. The stench had lingered on my equipment for weeks afterward. Somewhere, Ray must have waded in water contaminated with sulfide.

But there aren't any mines in the hills he'd been searching. I folded the jeans carefully and slid them back into their bag. Then I scanned the plat more closely.

He'd been methodical, moving from the north, section by section. I'd been in those hills, of course; I used to run in them when I was a girl. The section he'd apparently been working was in a valley, but he couldn't have gotten in there. It was completely fenced off because of . . .

Sinkholes.

There were four or five of them back there, craters from 60 to 150 yards across, roughly 80 feet deep, open pits carved out of the hills by an underground river. They've been fenced off for years because the footing's dangerously unstable. It seemed an unlikely place to hide a body. If you threw it down, it'd be visible from the rim. And even if you risked your neck to climb down to bury it, the crater floors were mostly moss and would show any disturbance.

Except for the largest of them. A branch of the river ran across the floor of the pit . . . and disappeared into the hillside. Anything dropped into it would be swept underground for several miles until the river surfaced again south of the hills and emptied into Thunder Bay. But if it was weighted? Maybe a weighted body would be carried underground, and would remain there.

That had to be it. That water was tainted with sulfide and Ray had said he might need my help later. He must have intended to search the riverbed where it disappeared underground, and he'd gotten wet wading around down there, scouting the area.

And then someone had shot him.

But it couldn't have happened at the sinkholes. The roads back to the holes were little more than tracks. He could never have driven out of there after he'd been wounded. Charlie was right—it must have happened closer to town. . . . I had a sudden flash of one person Ray would have let get close to him: a cop. A cop could have flagged him down anywhere along the road. And stepped close enough to shoot him. Nance? Possibly, or . . . maybe a cop who used to be an old football buddy of Owen McClain's.

Either way, it would explain a lot. How Ray's brother had disappeared so easily, and why the army had never been able to find Owen. He could have stayed a step ahead of them all the way.

Well, maybe I could change that. Until now, Owen's best camouflage had been that no one believed he was still alive and in the area. But there was proof, a body of evidence. And perhaps I even knew where it had been hidden. And if I could find Jimmy Calderon's body, it would flush Owen and the people who were protecting him into the light like the cockroaches they were.

41
THE PIT

─────────────────

⤲⤳

THE ROADS back to the holes were even worse than I remembered, barely more than twisting, potholed tracks. My Jeep would have managed with no problems, but Red's battered pickup truck lurched and jerked the whole way. Twice I slipped off the trail altogether and had to ease my way back on. The sky was clouding up to the north, but so far the rain was holding off, which was fortunate. I doubt I could have made it if the trails had been muddy.

I parked Red's truck at the end of the logging trail, near the rusty eight-foot chain-link fence that surrounded the sinkholes. There was a large gap in the fence, cut years ago, judging from the corroded ends of the severed wires. Kids, probably. You can't fence off curiosity, and most adventurous local kids had been back here at least once, including me. I'd explored the area with a gaggle of friends when I was fifteen or so.

We'd been disappointed. The sinks were literally just giant open holes, so large and obviously natural that they didn't seem particularly wondrous or mysterious, at least not to kids. Jack pines and aspen ringed the rims like sentries, and in a few spots trees clung like climbers stranded on rocky ledges. The crater floors were a camouflage blend of moss and patches of swamp grass, ocher and autumn gold.

The largest hole was different, though. A finger of the Thunder River surged to the surface roughly a third of the way across the floor of the crater, glittering like mercury in the afternoon sun. I guessed it was twenty feet across. It bisected the pit for seventy yards or so, then disappeared into a pool at the base of the hole's southwest wall.

I stepped carefully to the crater rim directly above the river's exit, wary of the footing. The soil was red clay covered with a slippery layer of pine needles. I'm no Danielle Boone, but someone had obviously been here recently. Ray? Possibly.

The drop to the river was sheer, a free fall of 150 feet. You wouldn't have to carry a body down; you could just push it over the rim and let the current do the rest.

I'd brought along a three-hundred-foot coil of nylon rope, thinking I'd have to lower my diving gear to the crater floor, but it wasn't necessary. A section of the rim had collapsed since I was here last, forming a ramp to the bottom of the pit, steep, but walkable.

I strapped on my air-tank backpack, slung the duffel bag with the rest of my gear over one shoulder, the coil of nylon line over the other, and worked my way down.

It was a rough go, the footing steeper than it appeared from above, especially since I was loaded down with what felt like a ton of gear. I paced myself, pausing several times to catch my breath and scan the area. The view was heart-stopping: cloud castles scudding across the open bowl of the moss-draped cliffs. But its beauty was diminished for me, because Ray might never see it again—or anything else. If he lived.

And then I noticed the footprints. Slight depressions were visible in moss and clay. I knelt and examined them. The edges were sharp, unsoftened by the rain earlier in the week. Someone had definitely been down here. Ray. This was the place then. It had to be.

At the hospital and afterward, I'd been numb, shocked into

exhaustion by what had happened to Ray. But as I worked my way down into the pit, I felt my spirit and my energy level rekindling, fueled by an icy anger I've felt only a few times in my life. A killing rage.

The river roiled and eddied when it met the cliff face, forming a pool. It didn't look deep, probably no more than eight to ten feet. I couldn't be sure, because the water was the color of café au lait, clouded with sulfide seepage from the shattered rocks. The foul reek of it was much stronger down here, held close by the walls. It was a rank stench of decay, as though the sinkhole were an open wound in the earth and gangrene had set in.

The current looked steady but not too fast; working in it would be no problem. My dive plan was simple: I'd anchor the nylon cable to one of the stunted jack pines near the pool's edge, then let the river carry me underground. If I was right, I shouldn't have to go very far. This current would move a weighted body only twenty or thirty yards at most. Still, the idea of actually being beneath the earth was sobering. It would be like swimming down into an open grave.

As I grimly pulled on my dry suit, tanks, and weight belt, I must have come up with a dozen perfectly sound reasons to quit; to get help, to come back another day. But each time I countered it with an image of Ray, smiling as we talked, looking into my eyes. Something he might never do again. And I knew if his brother was down here, I had to find him. I just had to.

I waded slowly into the river, up to my chest, then knelt and double-checked my regulator. Everything was A-OK. I was wearing a double tank, so I had plenty of reserve air. There was no reason to delay, and yet I hesitated. I took a long last look at the sky and the stunted tree I'd lashed the nylon cable to. And then I sank slowly into the water and let the current take me.

It was like swimming in a mist. The sunlight reflected off the hazy water and set it aglow with an milky fluorescence, limiting visibility to three feet or less. But the light held no warmth, the water was icy, and the chill, steady current seemed to suck life from me. Or maybe it was fear that made me shiver.

I stayed down near the bottom, circling the pool a few feet above the riverbed, scanning the rocks, stumps, and forest debris. No algae or reeds grew here; no fish swam. The sulfide made this stretch of river as dead as . . . the young man I'd come here to find.

But he wasn't here. I found no trace of him in the hazy pool. If he was in this place, the river must have carried him farther on, into the darkness of the underworld beneath the hills. I could almost feel the weight of all that soil and stone crouched above the cave mouth, ready to collapse again to form a new and larger sinkhole. With me beneath it. And I knew that if I hesitated for even a moment now, I'd turn tail and swim for the light.

I didn't. I couldn't. Instead, cursing my luck and my own damned stubbornness, I switched on my helmet lamp and thrust forward into the shadowy mouth of the cave. Into the darkness. And then the earth fell away.

I'd been quartering back and forth across the riverbed, scanning literally almost every inch of it, seeing nothing but debris, stones, and a few river crabs skittering about. The sudden downward slope shouldn't have surprised me; this river had already wreaked major havoc on the land about it, but the development did make me stop to reconsider my situation.

I'd assumed the river flowed beneath the hills more or less in a direct line to the lake, that my search would be restricted to a relatively narrow area. But the riverbed was dropping rapidly now, angling downward and widening out into a huge subterranean pool. A new sinkhole in the making.

My grip tightened involuntarily on my nylon lifeline. In a cavern this large, I could no longer trust the current for my sense of direction. If I lost the line, I could easily become disoriented and . . . And then I saw James Calderon's corpse.

42
JIMMY

I SHOULD have guessed he was near. I'd been seeing the little river crabs scuttling below me without realizing what it meant. There was no prey for them to hunt down here. Nothing lived here. They could only be eating carrion.

Jimmy'd come to rest on his side in a wide depression in the riverbed, a natural trap. His body was moving, or seemed to be. It was seething with small river crabs, dozens of them, crawling over him, and each other. Feeding.

I turned away, my mouth tasting a sudden surge of bile. I forced it down, composing myself, letting the current swing me away from him a little.

I checked my watch, trying to calculate how far I'd come from the cavern mouth. I'd been down eighteen minutes, but I'd been quartering back and forth rather than swimming in a straight line. I wasn't sure how far I'd actually traveled. Thirty to forty yards, maybe a little more. I'd come too far to haul the corpse back out against the current alone; I'd need help.

Or at least that's what I told myself. But even if I couldn't recover the body, I would still have to examine it carefully where it lay, to learn what I could about what had happened to him.

Sweet Jesus. I just couldn't. But I had to. There was no one else.

I bit down hard on my mouthpiece, using the pain to focus my concentration. Then I kicked gently and floated slowly back to Jimmy's corpse. The crabs were the worst of it, crawling over him like submarine maggots. I couldn't even brush them off without roiling the silt and reducing what little visibility I had. I'd have to look past them.

There was almost nothing left of the boy I'd met. His leather jacket had protected his torso, but most of the skin of his hands and face had been chewed away. A few patches of his long dark hair were still attached, waving gently in the current. The rest of his skull was cleaned nearly to the bone, with only odd bits of tendon and gristle still adhering to it. His eye sockets were empty save for tiny crabs scrabbling over one another to get inside.

The cause of death was clear enough. His skull was crushed, fractured by what must have been a series of powerful blows. So much for the auto-accident theory. The body'd been wrapped in a covering of some sort—heavy dark cloth that trailed off behind it in the current. Something about that shroud bothered me. It seemed familiar somehow. The pattern? I couldn't make it out clearly enough to be sure, but there was definitely something about it that nibbled at the corner of my memory. Maybe it would come to me later. The body was weighted by a single cinder block lashed to his legs with thin nylon cord. . . .

Sash cord—the kind used to draw drapes. That's what Jimmy's shroud was, a section of curtain. In the milky murk, I couldn't be positive, but I was fairly sure I'd seen the pattern before—in the McClain house.

He couldn't have been killed there; both Megan and Audrey had seen him leave. But whoever'd killed him obviously had access to the house . . . and for a split second I heard Hannah saying she'd been surprised when Audrey said Ross was out. "He's always sucking around . . ." Ross, with his dyed hair and sculpted

204

weight lifter's build. And somehow, Charlie had missed him. Or had he?

I needed that curtain. It was the kind of proof that couldn't be argued away. At the very least, it would connect Jimmy's murder to the house. Fortunately, the river had already done most of the work for me. The current had tugged the bulk of the material free, trailing it out along the floor of the trench. Only a corner of it was still connected to the body, trapped under the cord. I had my diving knife, of course, but I couldn't sever the cord that held the drape without cutting the body loose, as well. Damn.

There was no other way. I'd have to pull it free. I hooked the lifeline to my belt, then grasped the torn remains of Jimmy's calf with my left hand and tried to tug the drape from beneath the cord. Instantly, the world closed in as the silt roiled up around me. I felt crabs scrabbling across my hands, but the damned drape wouldn't move.

I jerked harder, and everything disappeared completely. Black water. I couldn't see anything at all.

I yanked furiously at the drape, tugging at it like a terrier. And suddenly, I felt it give. I inched it from beneath the cord until finally it slipped free. Got it! I released Jimmy's leg, took a firm grasp of my lifeline, and waited for the current to carry away enough of the silt so I could see again.

I was panting, shaking with exhaustion, as much from the tension and fear as from the effort involved. But gradually, I managed to get my breathing under control, and the hazy silt slowly cleared away. And I was sorry it did.

My struggle with the drape had rolled Jimmy's body over, and he faced me now, in all his ghastly horror. Lord of the crabs. Beast of black water.

Hell would be like this. I had to get out of here. I wrapped the the end of drape firmly around my wrist and yanked it free of the river bottom. And a second body exploded up at me out of the muck!

I ran! Or tried to. I scrambled frantically across the riverbed, banging off stumps, roiling the silt into a swirling tornado of black water. I forgot to swim, forgot everything in blind panic, fleeing like the hounds of hell were after me, trying to get away, trying to . . .

I slammed into something in the dark. A boulder? The cavern wall? I couldn't tell. I couldn't see anything but the swirling murk in front of my mask. And I was too afraid to grope, to reach out into the blackness, terrified I might be . . .

Might be what?

Grabbed? Clutched in the rotting arms of a corpse? No, not a corpse. It hadn't been a corpse. It was a . . . skeleton. Bones. Not a ghost or a monster. Just bones.

So it couldn't have lunged at me. I must have pulled it out of the silt with the damned drape. The drape. In my panic, I'd lost it, but it couldn't have gone far. It would be near the . . . bodies. My God. The horror . . .

I closed my eyes, willing myself to calm down, to slow my breathing. Get a grip, girl. Get a grip. Settle down.

All right. Okay. First of all, where was I? I made myself grope tentatively around the rock I'd banged into. There seemed to be no wall beyond it, so I was still in the riverbed. All I had to do was sit tight a few minutes and let the current carry the silt away and I'd be able to see again.

I still had my lifeline, and twenty minutes of air. I was all right for now. No call for a coronary. I'd come down here looking for Jimmy Calderon. And I'd found someone else as well, that's all. A second body. The question was: Whose?

Gradually, the silt I'd roiled up in my flight cleared away and I could see the river bottom. I took a deep breath, sucked up every shred of determination I had left, and then slowly worked my way back across the rocks to the bodies.

There wasn't much left of the second corpse. It had fallen to pieces when I'd pulled it up. Many of the smaller bones had simply vanished into the ooze at the bottom of the trench. The skull seemed to be that of an adult, but beyond that, I really couldn't tell much, whether it was man or a woman, how old, or even how tall. Perhaps it could be identified with dental records . . . if I brought the skull out with me.

I didn't like the idea much, but I didn't see any alternative. I felt gently around the base of the skull to see if it was still attached. And something icy crawled over my wrist. I recoiled, gasping; but I made myself try again. And then I saw it.

A strand of chain was tangled in the bones of the rib cage. Instantly recognizable. The older corpse was wearing a dog tag chain. I traced the narrow wire into the silt with my fingertips and found the tabs in the mud. They were black in the pale glow of my headlamp, too corroded to be legible, pitted and discolored by the sulfide. An electrochemical bath might restore them, but it really didn't matter. They'd obviously been down here a long time. And I was fairly sure I knew whose name was on them.

I took a last look at the trench where Jimmy Calderon and . . . the other had come to rest. The drape lay just beyond them, tangled in some debris. It was stable for now. The water was still too roiled to see much more. I could search it more carefully when we came back to recover the bodies. It was time to go. But I didn't.

I'd done all I could do for now, and God knows, it was a terrible place to be, yet I found myself oddly reluctant to depart. I hated the idea of leaving Jimmy here, of abandoning him in this reeking pit under the earth.

I'd met him only once, briefly, and hadn't liked him much. But God, he didn't deserve to end like this. No one does. I'll be back, I promised silently. I'll get you out. And then I squared myself off with the current and began to work my way slowly upstream.

43
OUT OF THE DARK

MOVING UPSTREAM was harder than I expected. River current is deceptive. You quickly adapt to the constant pressure and get on with what you're doing; and you forget that every moment is a struggle. Your body unconsciously fights for balance and to hold your position as your invisible enemy, the seemingly gentle current, leeches away your strength and body heat. It happens so subtly that you don't realize how much energy you've spent, until you try to do something simple, like swim upstream. It was all I could do to tug myself forward on the line, a foot at a time.

It took me roughly ten minutes to make my way back to the mouth of the cave, and seeing the shimmer of diffused sunlight filtering into the milky water ahead was as fine as waking to a sunrise after a nightmare. I broke the surface and swam to the bank, clutched a trailing root, spat out my mouthpiece, and just hung on, head down, panting like a dog.

When I looked up, Megan Lundy was standing there, staring down at me. Her gaze was as lifeless as one of her sculptures. She was dressed for running in her faded gray sweat suit and Nike headband . . . and she was holding an ugly palm-sized automatic casually at her side. It wasn't pointed at me; it was just there.

"Come on out," she said. "You can't stay there."

I heaved myself up on the bank. She took a wary step back, but she needn't have worried. I was physically drained and I was burdened with nearly eighty pounds of gear. I unsnapped my tank pack and eased it to the ground. She tossed a pair of handcuffs to me.

"Put these on."

"A womyn in chains?" I said.

"Just do it."

I hesitated, then slipped on the cuffs and snapped them closed. She motioned me up the path with the gun.

"What about my gear?"

"Leave it. You can come back for it later. Let's go."

She followed me up the long earthen ramp to the rim of the hole, keeping a watchful distance between us. "Charlie will never buy another accident," I said. "If something happens—"

"Shut up," she said cooly. "I'm trying to think."

"All I'm saying is—"

"If you don't shut your mouth, I swear I'll kill you, Mitch. I've got nothing to lose at this point."

I couldn't argue with that. But I decided if she tried to push me over the edge of the hole, I wasn't going down alone, gun or no gun.

But she didn't. At the top, she just motioned me toward Red's old pickup. "You drive," she said. She waited for me to get behind the wheel, then eased onto the seat beside me. I couldn't see the gun anymore, but I didn't have to.

"Where to?" I said, firing up the truck.

"My place, I think," she said. She sounded distant, lost in thought. I dropped the pickup into drive and started down the hill.

We rode in silence for several miles. I tried to catch sight of the gun, but she apparently was holding it next to her thigh.

209

With my hands in cuffs, I could barely manage the truck. I had no chance even to try for the gun.

"Did you find what you were looking for down there?" she said abruptly. Her voice had changed. It was forceful now, more at ease. I guessed she'd made a decision. About me? God only knew.

"Yes," I said cautiously, "I did. More than I was looking for, in fact."

"You mean Owen? He's still down there?"

"Sort of."

"I see," she said slowly. "I thought by now . . . Well, I guess it doesn't matter. He was a pig, you know, as sorry a bastard as ever walked the earth."

"What happened?" I asked.

"He found us together," she said quietly. "Audrey and me, in bed. I was just a kid, really, twenty or so. I'd come out here to go to college. And I was . . . troubled, unsure of my sexuality. And then I met Audrey at a fund-raiser, and . . . all of my questions were answered. She was the first person I ever truly loved. She was married, she was pregnant, and it didn't matter. It was an incredibly sweet awakening, for both of us.

"Then Owen . . . burst in on us in the middle of the night. He was on the run, half-drunk, terrified. When he found us together, he went berserk. He attacked Audrey. She tried to get away from him and fell down the stairs. And I . . . killed him. Stabbed him with a pair of shears. Half a dozen times, probably—I can't remember it very clearly.

"Audrey was badly hurt; bleeding. But she wouldn't let me call an ambulance. She knew what would happen to me if I did. A gay woman, killing her lover's husband? In those days, I wouldn't have had a chance, or now, either, for that matter. Not in this part of the country.

"I couldn't drive, so she had to. She drove up into these hills, to a place she knew. And then she drove all the way back to the house. And only then did she call an ambulance. She told them she'd had a bad fall. And then she made me leave her."

"My God," I said softly.

"She did it for me," she continued, as though I hadn't spoken. "She lost her baby, she nearly lost her life, trying to protect me. Later, she sent me off to school in New York. And I went on to have a career, and she . . . stayed behind. In her chair."

"A woman in chains," I said.

"Very perceptive," she said. "I know when you look at her now, the chair is really what you see. A broken, aging woman who's getting a little drifty, who's so twisted, she can barely turn her head. But to me, she was everything—is everything, my love, my art, everything. So when she called that night, half out of her mind, and said Owen had come back—"

"Owen?"

"She was distraught, not making any sense. But I could hear shouting in the background. I didn't know what to think. I grabbed a golf club, the first thing that came to hand. And I ran down the beach to the McClain house. I could hear him roaring as I ran up the porch steps. God, he even sounded like Owen. He was yelling at her, only an inch from her face, and she was in tears . . . and I hit him from behind with everything I had."

She fell silent. I didn't say anything. There was nothing to say.

"I'm not sure I meant to kill him," she continued after a bit. "I mean, I didn't even know who he was then. I just saw him screaming at Audrey and I . . . tried to protect her, I guess. Pure instinct. But to be honest, given the same circumstances, I'd do it again.

"Afterward, I . . . loaded him into his car, drove up into the hills, and pushed him over. And then I ran his car into the river. To hell with him. From what I've heard since, he wasn't much of a loss.".

"And his brother? To hell with him, too?"

"No," she said slowly. "I . . . regret what happened to him. I gave him those sketches hoping he'd either get discouraged or might stir up the locals enough that someone would drive him off. I even had a former student send him a cable from Toronto. Nothing worked. He wouldn't quit."

"So you fired the shots at the boat?"

"That was Audrey's idea—a bad one, I might add," she said, shaking her head. "I aimed in the general direction of the boat. I never dreamed I'd hit anything. And then I burned his car. We were desperate . . . Well, it doesn't matter now. I've been running in the hills, keeping track of Ray from a distance, hoping against hope that he'd give up, or simply miss it. And then yesterday, when he found the pit . . . I had no choice."

"So you waved him down. And he stopped, because he thought you were a friend. And you shot him," I said. "Just like that."

"No, not just like that!" she snapped. "My God, do you think I wanted any of this! I have a life; my art is *valued* by a great many people. I couldn't just throw it all away over a pig like Owen, or some sniveling little convict. I only did what I had to. I defended myself, and Audrey."

"I guess I can follow your logic as far as it goes," I said evenly. "I'm not sure Ray will find it much comfort. If he lives."

"I said I regret that, and I do. The odd thing is, I think if I'd killed him outright, it wouldn't trouble me as much as . . . what happened."

"Blinding him, you mean?"

"Yes," she said quietly. "To lose your sight . . . I swear to God, Mitch, I don't see how men do it."

"Do what?"

"Slaughter one another over nothing—over politics or territory or religion. They bomb cities, maim children. How can they possibly live with themselves afterward?"

"You seem to be doing all right."

"Yes," she said quietly. "I suppose I am. Pull in here."

We'd arrived at her home. I parked beside the house.

"We're going to walk around back to the studio," she said. "You first. Please don't do anything stupid."

"What are you going to do with me?" I asked.

"I don't know. I need to think."

She was lying. She'd decided my fate back on the road. I'd heard it in her voice. But she still had the gun, and she obviously wasn't afraid to use it. And I was still in cuffs and so exhausted that it was all I could manage to climb the spiral staircase up to the deck. Megan unlocked the studio and motioned me inside; then she moved quickly around the room, drawing the drapes.

"I'm going to lock you in," she said, "but I'll be where I can see you. Just sit tight. I'll be back in a few minutes." She backed out and closed the door. I heard the lock click shut, then her footsteps cross the deck. Then nothing.

Moving as quietly as I could, I frantically searched the studio, first for a weapon, then the keys to my handcuffs. The weapon was easy, such as it was. I found a bag of golf clubs in a closet and grabbed a putter out of it. It was no match for a pistol, but better than nothing. But I couldn't find the damned keys. There were chains and manacles everywhere, but no keys.

And then I saw the statue. Ashtoreth? Was that what she'd called it? But it wasn't. This time, I recognized it. It was Audrey. Young and beautiful and pregnant. And suddenly, everything that Megan had told me, and the things she hadn't, crystallized. And I realized what would happen now.

I carefully lifted the corner of the blind and scanned the deck. It was empty. No one in sight. I used the club to smash open the French door and let myself out. I dropped to all fours, crawled to the railing, then warily peered over the edge.

But there was no need for caution. Her running suit was folded neatly on the beach. The gun was lying on it. And Megan was nearly two hundred yards offshore, swimming steadily out toward . . . Nothing. The nearest land was the Canadian shore, 150 miles away.

"Megan!" I shouted.

And she heard me. She turned and faced me for a moment, treading water. And she raised both hands in the air, her fists clenched. A salute? A good-bye? She turned and swam on.

I sprinted down the steps, smashed in her front door, and used the phone to call 911. Then I charged back to the beach, but . . .

There was nothing to see. Thunderclouds were rolling down from the north, roughing up a chop that was already a foot or so high. I didn't need binoculars to know she was gone. There wasn't even a ripple to show where she'd been. The bay stretched away, dark and empty. Black water, all the way to the horizon.

44
ASHTORETH

RAY SURVIVED the day. That night, a helicopter flew him down to U of M hospital. He was in surgery for nearly six hours. His condition is still serious, but he's going to live, and he may recover much of the vision in his right eye. I'll go down to visit him in a few days. I hope he'll be able to see me.

Charlie picked up Ross and grilled him and Ross folded like a house of cards. He admitted that Gordon had brought him here to con Owney out of whatever they could get. Charlie said the two creeps are so busy trying to incriminate each other that he'll probably solve the Kennedy assassination before they're through.

Megan left a letter behind that stated, more or less, what she'd told me. And Charlie accepted it at face value and closed the investigation. But we both know it wasn't true. At least not all of it. Megan couldn't have taken Jimmy's body up into the hills in his rental car. She didn't drive.

She may have been able to manage the short trip to the river; I suppose any unskilled driver could do that much. But even if she'd been able to handle the difficult drive into the hills, Jimmy's little rental Escort could never have made it back to those holes.

Someone else helped her take the body up there, and only one person could have: Audrey. In the van modified for her wheelchair, the vehicle only she could drive.

If Charlie'd checked her van, he probably would have found bloodstains in it. But he didn't. Because it didn't matter anymore.

The night Megan disappeared, Audrey had a stroke. Hannah says she's fading quickly, as though she's given up. I think she means to follow Megan wherever she has gone, into the depths of black water, or whatever lies beyond.

I still have the Ashtoreth carving I took from Megan's house. I meant to give it to Audrey. It's hers by right. But in her present condition, I'm not sure how she'd react.

No. That's only partly true.

The truth is, there's something about this rude clay figure that haunts me. She's rising from primordial waters, her belly is swollen, and her breasts are full. Her eyes seem to hold an unvoiced message for me, even though they're more implied than realistic. Her hands are upraised, fists clenched. A victory salute of ultimate triumph. It was the gesture Megan Lundy made to me from the lake. A good-bye, a final plea for understanding. Before she turned and swam away into forever.

I have been in love, and I have been loved, I think. But I know in my heart, I have never felt the depth of passion embodied in this elemental bit of art. To kill for someone. To willingly die to protect them. I know I've never loved anyone that much. Perhaps I never will. And yet, I know now that such love does exist. Ashtoreth is the evidence.

The carving is deceptively crude, perhaps in homage to the countless earth goddesses found in tombs all over the world. Or perhaps it's simply unfinished. And now, it always will be.

The figure isn't physically recognizable as Audrey, but I know it's her. Free of her chair. And her body, and her years. Somehow, Megan captured the image of her soul: a woman unchained.

And the truth is, I'm not sure now that I would give it to Audrey, or anyone, even if I knew beyond doubt that it was the right thing to do.

Because, aside from my son, newborn, with afterbirth still matted in his hair . . . Megan's goddess is the most beautiful thing I have ever seen.

After the "accidental" death of her estranged father, Mitch Mitchell returns home to the small town of Huron Harbor, Michigan—and finds that he was involved in some very lethal business.

She suspects the worst: her father was murdered. And before he died, he was gripped by fear. Why else was he keeping loaded guns inside his isolated cottage and planning a drastic move to Baja? Soon Mitch is digging into his shady past and discovering shattering secrets about her family—and a shocking plot that threatens her very life.

ICEWATER MANSIONS

DOUG ALLYN